WINDOWS OF HEAVEN

Christian Pascale

Aster Press
Blue Fortune Enterprises, LLC

For information contact :
Blue Fortune Enterprises, LLC
Aster Press
P.O. Box 554
Yorktown, VA 23690
http://blue-fortune.com

Cover design by Odd Moxie

ISBN: 978-1-948979-61-0
First Edition: January 2022

Dedication

To my wife Liria
and my two sons, Raphael and Michel

ACKNOWLEDGEMENTS

This book is the result of two years of continuous and persistent effort. I could not have done it alone. Sometimes it takes a village, and my village has been the members of the Williamsburg Writers Group. Their patience and constructive criticism were invaluable in helping me clarify themes and content.

I would like to thank my wife for her patience and encouragement and my sons for their confidence in my ability to convey a message that readers would find entertaining as well as instructive.

I deeply appreciate the help of my friend, editor, and publisher, Narielle Living. Without her advice and encouragement, this book would not have come to fruition.

Dear Reader,

When you open the pages of this novel, I hope you will find something for which you are searching.

Those of you, who believe, as I do, that our future is in danger and that we are the caretakers of the earth, will find described in this novel the potential dystopian future we all fear. However, it is never too late.

Those who simply want to be entertained by a fast-moving adventure story with lots of sound and fury will not be disappointed.

A third group of readers with perhaps a more philosophical view of life will see in this book an allegory resembling French writer Albert Camus' *La Peste (The Plague)*. Evil in this book is not a plague, but something else. This book challenges the reader to decide how to destroy the evil that runs rampant in our world.

Enjoy,

Christian Pascale

"...if I will not open you the windows of heaven and pour you out a blessing that there shall not be room enough to receive it."

Malachi 3:10

PROLOGUE

A wave of terror swept through everyone as an incoming asteroid about two kilometers in size broke apart in the earth's atmosphere. The silence was surprising but not unexpected from an object hurtling through space at such a high speed. One piece hit a deserted area in the Siberian tundra. It threw up a massive dust cloud, obliterating the sun but avoiding a major population center. Before the world could breathe a sigh of relief, the second part of the asteroid, a kilometer in length, smashed into the Gulf of Mexico. The collision set off a series of catastrophic underwater earthquakes and seismic activity, which affected the earth's tectonic plates and resulted in several Category Five hurricanes. Massive tsunamis struck the shores of every continent, and coastal cities disappeared. Darkness descended for a brief time.

At the time of the event, Labor Day, September 2050, scientists estimated that the asteroid strike, combined with previous drastic climate change, was equivalent to the effect of all the ice on earth melting at once. The sea, like Noah's flood, engulfed the land. Ocean levels rose 300 to 350 feet. The asteroid strike, along with extremely active volcanos, produced enough atmospheric dust to block forty percent of the sun's rays. The ever-expanding ash cloud chilled the earth, already overheated by greenhouse gas emissions.

Many were lost.

Many mourned.

Many felt it might be the beginning of another ice age.

Chapter 1

As Tom Rogers waited for his sister, the dust-covered sun disappeared as night blanketed the snowy ground. Mesmerized by the sight, Tom recalled *The Garden of Time*. The story described a magic garden on the grounds of a castle, home to a count and countess. In the distance, a dark, disorderly multitude approached. Each day, as the menacing mob drew nearer, the Count picked a crystal bud from the stem of one of his last magic flowers. The horde immediately returned to its former position. Tom wished he, too, could pluck such a crystal rose and go back in time, reverse the last day, last month, last year. He longed to feel the sun's warmth touching his skin as he sat by the sea on a sandy beach at low tide on a summer's day in Duck, North Carolina. Unfortunately,

Tom remembered, the Count and Countess finally ran out of flowers.

Lost in his somber thoughts, Tom zipped his ski jacket to protect himself against the cold. In 2050, mid-September now resembled former late December. He wore jeans, a three-colored flannel shirt, and a clashing woolen scarf he had found in an abandoned dorm room. A worn blue ski hat covered his unruly brown hair. His electric razor was useless, and he had been unable to locate a regular safety razor. Several weeks of beard growth showed a mixture of brown and reddish stubble. He had never been able to grow a moustache; the area over his mouth looked like he had wiped a dirty hand across his upper lip.

As he stood on the bluffs overlooking College Avenue, Tom's piercing blue eyes surveilled the town of Easton. After Surge Saturday, the Delaware River had become a bay stretching to the east and covering the area where Philadelphia once stood. With nightfall approaching, Tom hoped his sister, Helene, would return quickly. She would be climbing College Avenue and soon it would be too dark to see her. During these precarious times, he tried to keep an eye on her as best he could, even though she was technically an adult.

Tom reached for the Total Nuts candy bar he had slipped into the front pocket of his pants. He had rummaged through his car for half an hour and found only the one bar. The hybrid car that ran on gas, electric or solar battery sat useless. There were no functioning charging stations, little sun, and no gas station with working pumps in the Easton area.

His jeans felt tight, and then he remembered the small New Testament in his back pocket. His mother had given him the book several years ago, and he still cherished the gift. Now, he wondered how long it would be before its prophetic visions all came true. Pulling it out in the failing light, he reread underlined words from the Gospel of Luke: *And there shall be signs in the sun, and in the moon, and in the stars; and upon the earth distress of nations, with perplexity; the sea and the waves roaring. Men's hearts failing them for fear... The sun shall be turned into darkness, and the moon into blood... (Luke 21-25)*

He shivered as he contemplated the future. *The earth's ice caps have substantially melted, the waves of the sea have roared, volcanoes have spewed fire, nations have been in great distress, and an asteroid split into two pieces, striking the earth. We lost so many. Men's hearts have begun to fail for fear. What is next?*

Chapter 2
A History Lesson

Tom had majored in world history at Virginia Tech and graduated in 2048. He remembered from a class on Environmental History that in the early part of the twenty-first century, scientists found proof in Iceland of a connection between the end of the glaciers in 5500 BC and the rise of volcanic activity. As the glaciers melted, the earth warmed, volcanos threw ash into the sky, and the ash cloud shut out the sun. The world became dark, cold, and this created a mini Ice Age. This era lasted until the glaciers grew again, volcanic activity stopped, the sky cleared, and the earth basked in the warming sun. Was this vicious circle beginning again?

Approximately seven thousand years later, in May

1780, settlers in North America believed the end of the world had arrived. The sun and moon glowed red, the sky turned to yellow, and by noon, there was a perpetual night lasting for more than a day. This was no solar eclipse, no volcanic eruption, just forest fires and resultant ash which blocked out sunlight. It was not the end of the world, simply a taste of what was to come.

In 2019, the majority of world scientists ratcheted up their warnings to people about what was happening and the possibility of dire consequences. That same year, rivers in the Northwest United States warmed and salmon could not spawn. Aquatic species in the cold artic waters began to disappear, and surface layers of water in Siberia, 200 miles north of the Arctic Circle, were no longer freezing. Within a year, the temperature in the area reached 100 degrees Fahrenheit, a record high. A rise in volcanic activity in Greenland caused eleven billion tons of ice to melt in just one July day. Land in Canada, which not been seen in forty thousand years, reappeared as the glaciers melted. In the Novoya Zemlya Archipelago, a Russian scientist discovered five new islands uncovered by the melting ice of the Vyliki glacier. In July, a heatwave produced fires that raged over Siberia and burned down an area as large as Greece. The fires released some 56 million tons of carbon dioxide and huge amounts of greenhouse gases. Seventeen million square miles of permafrost melted.

In the early 2020s, seeing signs of grave environmental change, some scientists predicted that by 2100 the rising oceans would displace over one fifth of the world's population. Other more optimistic scientists felt that there was still plenty of time to save the earth and said it would take five thousand years for all the world's ice to melt and the ocean water level to rise sufficiently to inundate the world's coastal cities. Eventually, these optimists were proven wrong.

Governments at the time would not believe the evidence of melting glaciers, warming waters, stronger storms, more active volcanos, larger floods, and dangerous droughts. Some selfishly pulled out of the World Climate Accord or gave it token acceptance and refused to reduce fossil fuels. Brazil and China, among others, permitted environmental damage to fuel economic progress. China's economic zones, pollution in India, and Brazil's destruction of the Amazon rain forest contributed to the eventual environmental disaster.

By 2040, the release of carbon dioxide and greenhouse gases heated the atmosphere by over five degrees Celsius and the world that existed gradually ended. The sea level, predicted to rise by three feet in a worst-case scenario, rose by four. Cold zones started to become temperate, temperate zones turned dry and deserts began to expand. The breadbaskets of the world began to change, causing a shift in population, migration from island nations, an increase in world hunger, and fights over water rights.

The pandemic that began in 2042 mirrored what had transpired in an earlier decade: 2020. However, the world's collaborative effort in 2020 (which unfortunately did not lead to cooperation on global warming) was not repeated. In a move reminiscent of 2020, nations spent a year on lockdown isolated from each other before a cure was developed.

By early 2050, way before expected, a combination of the excessive melting of the polar caps, multiple earthquakes, and the continuing toll taken by the greenhouse gas effect caused the ocean water level to rise by an average of twenty feet.

In September 2050, when the asteroid hit, cities on the United States' eastern seaboard and along the Gulf of Mexico disappeared under 500-foot tsunami waves.

Chapter 3
Easton, Pennsylvania

As he waited for his sister on Lafayette Hill, Tom opened his Bible and flipped to the Book of Revelation. When he was a teen, his mother often quoted the verse he now read: *A great mountain burning with fire was cast into the sea… The third part of the sea became blood; and the third part of the creatures, which were in the sea, and had life, died; the third part of the ships were destroyed… the third part of the sun was smitten, and the third part of the moon, and the third part of the stars…*

On what came to be known as Surge Saturday, Labor Day, September 2050, as a result of the asteroid hit, a tsunami crashed over Washington, D.C., killing millions. Tom's parents, working overtime at their government jobs, were assumed among them. They were part of a government task force, which had been desperately trying to hold together the pieces of the failing federal government. On the day before, Tom's parents asked him to drive from his home in Blacksburg, Virginia to Lafayette College in Easton, Pennsylvania and pick up his younger sister, Helene. She was a sophomore and wanted to go home for the holiday. That Friday, Tom drove north, passing through the Blue Ridge Mountains on Route 81 and then moving east along Route 78 to Easton.

After Surge Saturday, Easton became waterfront property. The foothills of the Poconos had stopped the sea, but the former Delaware River was now part of a large bay surrounded by delta marsh. Easton was similar to Blacksburg, Tom's current home. Blacksburg nestled on a plateau between the Blue Ridge and the Allegheny mountains. The Blue Ridge stopped the water that rolled across Virginia from the coast, but the expansive Smith Mountain Lake was now part of an inland sea that stretched from Roanoke to what had once been Norfolk.

Tom was not yet aware of the extent the world had changed, but he was worried about his sister. When he arrived on Friday, she had asked about their mom and dad. Tom said he called that morning and they were fine. The next morning, they packed the car, preparing for an early start. Tom turned the key in the ignition, and the radio came on as well. Three long, unpleasant noises erupted, the signal for an announcement from the Emergency Alert System.

"We interrupt this broadcast with an emergency update from the Vice President of the United States."

Tom and Helene stared at each other, a sense of foreboding bubbling between them.

"My fellow citizens, it is with great sadness that I come to you today with news of a catastrophic event." The vice president paused, the silence broken only by the sound of her trying to catch her breath.

"Is she crying?" Helene whispered. Tom shook his head, uncertain.

Finally, she continued. "The city of Washington, D.C., along with other major East Coast metropolitan hubs, has been destroyed by massive tsunamis. We have lost contact with the President and Cabinet. Most members of the federal government, along with the president, are believed lost. I am speaking to you from the University of Virginia in Charlottesville. I will try to bring updates as I receive them. For now, stay calm and seek higher ground."

Helene immediately said, "Mom and dad are okay. They made it out. They'll call us."

Tom closed his eyes for a brief moment. *I must remain calm*, he thought. *I'll deal with my pain later. Right now, my sister needs reassurance.* He opened his eyes and looked at his sister with all the tenderness he could muster. "Maybe you're right, but it took out the greater D.C. area. It's now ocean. Still, we might hear from them."

After that, the world fell silent. Tom believed his parents to be dead, but he tried to hold himself together for his sister's sake. Helene, hysterical and crying every time the subject was broached, refused to accept what Tom knew to be fact. At this point, he could not bring himself to dash her belief that she would see their mom and dad again.

With their parents now missing, if not dead, Tom wanted to take Helene back to Blacksburg. However, catastrophic weather events—volcanic activity and ice and snow caused by the early beginnings of an oncoming new Ice Age—made travel over the last weeks too dangerous. So they stayed put in Easton, trying to wait out the weather and uncertain of their futures. In fact, uncertain of everyone's future. Lafayette College closed, and over the following weeks, it became the home to a forlorn group of former students and refugees living in their snowy citadel, separate from the city below. The inhabitants survived by using what food remained in the generator-run cafeteria freezers, but food supplies were now running low.

As he waited for Helene, Tom thought about a shortwave radio message from an Albuquerque station that he had listened to earlier in the day. What he had heard was pure Black Sun propaganda. *Those guys are dangerous fanatics. I definitely want to avoid them.* He had hoped that the acting President and the transitional government, which had been hastily set up in Albuquerque because that location had received the least amount of weather disruptions, would deal with this group. But the government now had no way of dealing with this new danger. The new capital of the United States, along with its weak transitional government, now in Albuquerque, New Mexico, had fallen to the paramilitary soldiers of the Black Sun.

Chapter 4
Black Sun

Hidden like a poisonous viper since the aftermath of World War II, this neo-Nazi movement rose again to greet the apocalyptic dawn. Their symbol, a black sun wheel, had a dark center with twelve radial runes, or Nordic letters with supposed magical properties. The runes existed in Northern Europe before the Latin alphabet and allegedly represented a mystical energy source that would renew the Aryan race. The ranks of these neo-Nazi extremists increased, beginning with the tacit approval of the U.S. political machine that held power in the mid-two thousands. These extremists became stronger as successive presidents fought with the U.S. Congress. Many congressional representatives secretly approved the Black Sun agenda and tried to push through legislation that would limit the rights of minority citizens and put power in the hands of those who supported Black Sun.

During the economic and ecological disasters, Black Sun continued to spread its nationalist-authoritarian ideology as they prepared to seize the moment. Leveraging the psychological power of their apocalyptic message, they silently stood in the streets, holding signs proclaiming Seize Your Power and encouraging the New Age movement to join them in their mission. They held simple dinners in empty halls, feeding people and focusing on not only the disenfranchised poor white people but also the lost spiritual seekers who could not see what the message truly meant.

Men with bullhorns spoke softly but were heard everywhere. "They're coming for you…" they proclaimed. "They're taking your rights."

Many believed them.

They blamed socialists and Jews for the economic depression, blacks for social unrest, and Africans and Hispanics for pouring into the U.S. and causing economic blight. At open rallies leaders spoke of God's coming destruction of earth, a result of His desire to punish non-apocalyptic Christians, as well as Muslims, socialists, and homosexuals. Black Sun leadership, communicating over short-wave radio, blamed the asteroid-caused environmental disaster on a dirty bomb supposedly set off by Islamic extremists.

They were wrong, but when a lie is told often enough, it becomes the truth, at least for those who want to believe it.

News of Black Sun's violent coup against the post-surge interim government in Albuquerque quickly spread to the new East Coast in mid-September. Over the years, the group had secretly penetrated high levels of the U.S. government and some held positions of command in the U.S. Army and in most National Guard units across the country. Black Sun's philosophy, *America First*, appealed to the masses. When the time came, they made sure no National Guard unit or Army division came to the aid of the beleaguered Federal Government. Those who opposed them were quickly eliminated.

Several days after Surge Saturday, three divisions of Black Sun troops, thirty-thousand men strong, marched into Albuquerque and took over the new U.S. capital. They declared a state of emergency with the Black Sun

Party as head of the new government. What was left of Congress and the Supreme Court were abolished. There was little opposition, which is what happens when a group spends years preparing.

Black Sun leaders put the Vice President, then acting President of the interim government and her advisors under house arrest, awaiting a trial for treason.

Black Sun established an eastern headquarters in Pittsburgh, which, despite its rivers, was far enough inland to avoid the floods. From there, it immediately began to exercise control over New York, Pennsylvania, and what was left of Maryland and Virginia and quashed all opposition. The Albuquerque Black Sun government moved quickly to seize the Strategic Petroleum Reserve in Austin, Texas.

As he waited for his sister, Tom remembered that a few days before, the party's symbol had appeared on one of the frozen college buildings. Their propaganda dominated the town and the communication media, which consisted of printed posters placed on walls. Every day, he tried looking for another radio station without success.

Chapter 5
Helene Returns

Later that evening, Helene made it back safely to their temporary apartment, which was a bare-essentials room. It contained two chairs, a desk, and two twin beds. Nothing else. There was an adjoining bathroom with a shower, but the water was cold. Tom looked at his sister, sitting on a bed, and turned his radio off.

"Did you listen to the shortwave today?" he asked. The tall, athletic-looking, raven-haired young woman shook her head. Helene was one of those girls everyone noticed. Her once tanned slender legs had grown pale. She had let her hair grow for some weeks before Tom arrived, and besides being much longer than she normally wore, it was now tangled and slightly greasy. Despite this, her striking beauty, highlighted by her emerald-green eyes and raised cheekbones, was in no way marred.

"No," she replied. "I was foraging for gas. If we can't generate energy, we have no heat. These buildings don't have wood-burning hearths, and we'll have to start burning furniture and opening windows. Don't know how long that will last."

"Don't the dorms have backup generators for electricity?" Tom asked.

"The dorms all have solar panels, and the main back-up generators are also solar with the sun's light used to charge the batteries. The solar generators have charge controllers producing direct current electricity accompanied by an alternate current invertors converting energy to the AC current that will run most electronic devices and the dorm's heating system. With the decrease in the light caused by the ash cloud, solar has not been a good option."

Helene twirled a piece of her hair in one hand, slouching forward as she spoke. "However, these are hybrid or tri-fuel generators which also work off of gas and natural gas. The natural gas system is in disarray, so we can't pipe that in, but we can use regular gas if we can find it. Most gas stations run off electricity and, with the electric grid down, they can't pump gas. But there must be vehicles left on the street downtown, some of which run on gas. I just haven't found any yet. Those people with cars that had at least a half tank probably left and went further south."

"You were always the practical one, sis," Tom said. "Even when we were young, you played at being the scientist and I was the dreamer. I remember how excited you were when you got your first computer with chemistry and physics programs loaded on it. You read Einstein. I read Shakespeare."

"You know I believe in science," she said. "It's what makes sense and what will keep us alive."

Tom stood and paced in the limited space. "Did you see any of those Black Sun symbols down in the town? I noticed some on the campus walls. I don't think anyone here put them there. It must be some group from Easton."

"Easton started as a factory town, and the new condos and yuppie types are just a thin veneer over the blue-collar core," Helene said. "The townsfolk could easily welcome Black Sun or join them. Many of them appear to share the same closed-minded philosophy."

"Let's get dinner at the cafeteria," Tom said. "I don't know if they have any frozen meat or chicken left that we can cook, but at least what faculty are here will be handing out cans of baked beans. A guy I know found a ton of those cans in a storeroom on the basement level. Luckily, I still have my Swiss Army knife with a can opener. Tomorrow I'll help you search for gas."

"Maybe we should organize the hill, form committees or something, provide for ourselves as a group. Our lives may now depend on each other," she said.

"No!" Tom replied. "We've got to get to Blacksburg. I know how to survive there, and I have a network of friends if they're still there. This life here is temporary. Besides, they seem to have already organized what's left of the food."

Chapter 6
Looking for Gas

The next morning around nine, as the sun began to thaw the frozen ground, Tom and Helene started their trek down College Avenue and into the town of Easton. They planned to look for old gas-run vehicles. When they arrived at Main Street, Tom suggested they look inside an abandoned men's barbershop where a sign hung by one hook and twisted in the wind. "If we can find some scissors, we can cut our hair," he said. Talcum powder was strewn over the dirty floor and mirrors had been smashed. Nothing was there, except for the design of a black sun wheel with a dark center drawn on the far wall with black marker. They left, knowing there was nothing for them.

As the wind grew colder, Tom turned to Helene. "You know this town better than I do. Where can we go to escape this frigid air?"

"There's a public library on Church Street," Helene said. "Maybe they have a generator and some heat. Also, we can see what books are left." They trudged down the few cold and windy blocks to Church Street and saw that the library doors were propped open. Inside, it was warm. Several fires had been started by using books as kindling and chairs as firewood. The smoke rose and the scent of burning paper filled the air. The men standing around them, many of whom had on Black Sun armbands, were too busy feeding the fires to notice Tom and Helene. Despite the evident danger, the two needed a moment to warm up. They kept to the shadows in the smoke-filled room and hid behind some tall bookshelves. As he peeked out from his hiding place, empty bookshelf sections loomed before him. He read the labels: History, Politics, Social Issues, and World Religions. The books were gone. The siblings moved behind a cart full of books labeled *for burning*. From his position, Tom reached over the top and casually grabbed a book. Its title was *Gay and Lesbian Rights in the Early 2000s.*

A shout almost caused Tom to drop the book. A

group of men in black uniforms and boots dragged two prisoners into the library. The prisoners' hands were tied behind their backs and placards hung around their necks. The younger man's placard read "homo" and the older man's "intellectual." Tom wanted to run, but his mind was filled with horror and his legs would not move. He needed to get Helene out of there.

The Black Sun insignias on the men's jackets stood out, a hostile image to any who disagreed. Both captives looked as if they were having trouble breathing, whether from fear or health crisis, Tom didn't know. The younger man was thin and tall. He hunched over in pain, his face crossed with blue welts and several teeth missing. Blood matted his long brown hair. The older man, in a tweed jacket with tailored sleeves now torn and ragged, raised his head as if to appeal for help from the heavens. As they pushed him forward, he fell to his knees. A rifle butt to his back got him on his feet again. With no electricity, the elevators were no longer functioning, and the group took the stairs to the top floor. Those Black Sun soldiers at the fires followed them with their eyes.

Taking the opportunity to escape, Tom and Helene quietly fled outside. As they slipped out the side door, they passed a poster for Hitler's *Mein Kampf* taped onto the outside of the door. Once on the street, they moved behind an abandoned vehicle.

A commotion from the library roof drew their attention upward. The prisoners hovered on the edge. Soldiers with guns stood behind them. Two of the soldiers raised the butts of their rifles and slammed them into the backs of the men, whose hands were still tied. Tom's horror grew as the men stumbled into thin air, gravity taking over. The siblings averted their eyes before the bodies hit the ground, but there was no mistaking the solid *thwack* of flesh on concrete.

We have to get out of here, Tom thought, and when he looked at Helene, she nodded, knowing what he was thinking. As they prepared to slip quietly away, another group of black-uniformed soldiers appeared, men and women, escorting two young women who also had their hands tied. Even though it was bitterly cold, they were naked from their waist up, and their faces were bruised. Their placard read, "dykes and lesbos." As the women entered the library, they passed the lifeless prisoners and began to scream and cry.

Trying not to be obvious, Tom and Helene quickly walked away. Their goal now was to find a car with gas, while avoiding the main streets. After three hours, they found nothing and sadly climbed back up the hill.

Tom and Helene were filled with fear. Fortunately, it was apparent that the Black Sun "liberators" had just arrived in Easton. Their men, trucks, and helicopters had not yet turned their attention to College Hill. The two wondered what awaited those on the campus who did not fit the Aryan profile of the "liberators."

Chapter 7
Food and a Vehicle

A week passed, and Black Sun continued to focus on the town. As the atrocities piled up, Tom worked to find transportation out of Easton as soon as possible. Back in their dorm room, the two spoke in whispers, afraid other residents would hear. "We can't wait much longer. If Black Sun takes over the college, it may be too late," Tom said.

"But what about our mom and dad? Lafayette is where they will try to find us. What if they come here?"

"We can't risk it. I know we will be safe at my place in Blacksburg. At least I know the terrain. I hope I'm right. One thing I know, we can't stay here."

He and Helene descended College Hill again, this

time in search of a vehicle with a least a half tank of gas, so they could drive farther south. Perhaps they could get as far as Virginia. They also needed to forage for any food remaining in the supermarket they had noticed during their last trip. Weaving quietly through back streets, they arrived at Washington Street, where the Northampton County Courthouse and the prison dominated the scene. As the siblings passed in front of the Courthouse, a flag with a Black Sun emblem waved from a pole and just beneath it, a gallows had been erected. A man and woman hung from the structure, their bodies swaying with the wind. The woman wore a hijab.

When Tom and Helene approached the supermarket, the distant sound of gunfire alerted them to trouble. They ducked into an alley to avoid encountering several men in uniforms. These black-uniformed soldiers carried a mix of what appeared to be SARs and Steyr assault rifles.

Nearing the market, the two smelled the stench of rotting food mixed with the smell of human feces. They found two metal rods thrown on a junk pile and picked them up for defense. Tom clutched the cold metal tightly, hoping he would have no cause to use it.

Turning a corner, they found themselves on the fringes of a firefight. Other black-uniformed soldiers fired at three African-American youths who were leaving the supermarket with bags of canned food. The taller youth with a black pencil mustache and a bushy afro held an old Taurus revolver. His face was a mix of terror and anger as he fired the weapon. He had been surprised, but this did not stop him from shooting and wounding one of the approaching soldiers in the arm. The anger in his eyes turned to despair as he tried to cram new cartridges into the cylinder. They shot him while he was reloading. The two younger boys, not more than sixteen and clean-shaven with short-cropped hair, continued to fire wildly, not hitting anyone. Their nine-millimeter handguns were no match for automatic assault weapons. They both fell, bodies torn apart by bullets coming at them from all sides in a rain of abomination.

"We gotta run quick," Tom whispered. "Forget the food and vehicle. It's getting way too dangerous. Our chances of finding a gas-run vehicle are slim in this town. Let's get back to campus. We can try later—maybe a farmer's truck or one of those special antique cars."

They took a circuitous route through small streets and back alleys until they arrived at College Avenue. Keeping their heads low, they jogged up the hill until they were safe inside the campus.

"That was too close," Helene said, out of breath from the run. "We need to consider leaving sooner rather than later."

"So now you agree, we need to leave?" Tom said.

Chapter 8
Easton's Bunker Hill

Two days later, after grabbing two cans of baked beans and stuffing what clothes they had in a duffle bag, they were ready to leave. They would need to find more food along the way. Food on campus was almost exhausted. Still hoping they could find a gas-run vehicle to take them south, Tom went to the campus bluff to see what was going on in the city and determine if they could try one more time to locate transportation. When he reached the overlook, he saw what looked like a hundred Black Sun soldiers proceeding slowly up College Avenue toward the campus. Two gas-run Humvees accompanied them.

Apparently, someone on campus had sounded an

alarm, as there were about forty civilians on the bluff. A young man dressed in khakis motioned at people as if he was in charge. Most people appeared not to pay attention to his directions and shouted out instructions. The bluff was in total chaos. Four people used a large catapult slingshot, the type fraternity pledges used to launch water balloons at other fraternity houses. Two held the sides of the device against opposite trees, while a third pulled back the slingshot. The fourth placed a large rock in the cradle and launched it into space. They managed to hit the closest soldiers, knocking two senseless. Several others on the bluff, armed with small arms, mostly revolvers and pistols, also hit a few soldiers. A third group of resistors filled bottles with precious gasoline, stuffed the openings with rags, then lit the rags and heaved the flaming missiles at the closest part of the column. The Black Sun soldiers came in range of their Molotov cocktails as they approached the last series of turns before the summit.

As Tom arrived on the scene, the gunner atop the first Humvee began rapid fire at the hilltop. Tom quickly retreated against the nearest building. At first, the gunner's bullets did not reach the ragged group. Civilians shouted, "Fuck Black Sun!" The taunting stopped, however, when the Humvees came within effective firing range and the bluff quickly resembled a combination of Bunker Hill and Tiananmen Square. Along the bluff, resistors fell like a deck of cards, one after the other, hit by rapid fire from the Humvees. The grass was stained with blood. Bodies missing arms and legs were strewn across the bluff. Within three minutes, the hilltop was empty. Those left standing were either too stunned to move or ran away in a panic for the shelter of the buildings, tripping over or stepping on the bodies of their fallen comrades. Tom saw a young girl wandering as if she were sleep walking. A bullet took off the top of her head. She fell to the ground, her arms still twitching.

Suddenly, the sky turned bright red, then became darker. The wind shrieked, small black tornados began to swirl through the town below, and hail the size of golf balls rained down. The soldiers and the protesters alike sought shelter, scurrying to buildings and empty vehicles as destruction rained upon them. Lightning flashed across the sky as an incarnation of human hate which struck indiscriminately.

The encounter ended. Tom returned to the apartment and told Helene what he had seen.

"I'm glad I was not there," she said. I don't think I could

have managed seeing all the chaos, blood and bodies."

The next morning, when Tom awoke and looked out the window, he could barely see the sun. Only sparse rays of sunlight managed to shine through the haze of dust in the atmosphere. However, the wind was calm and the storm had passed.

A voice boomed from a loudspeaker. "All Lafayette College inhabitants must report to the quad immediately." Tom and Helene jumped out of their beds in fear. *Who was that voice and why did they need to go to the quad?* With pajamas hidden under winter coats, they joined the crowd. Along the edge of the quad stood a line of black-clad soldiers, with one Humvee at each end. Tom tried to count the number of soldiers to avoid thinking about what was coming. An officer using a battery-powered loud speaker addressed the crowd.

"This campus is under martial law, as is the entire city of Easton. I represent the Arizona Black Sun Government. You are required to bring all your books here to this field where they will either be approved or burned. All firearms must be turned in. Food rationing will begin now, and all personal food supplies will be requisitioned."

Chapter 9
We Gotta Get Out of this Place

That night, Tom and Helene sat in their room in silence, lost in thought. Black Sun soldiers had been by the dorm earlier to search for weapons and take what food was there. As Tom pondered their future, a song that had been a favorite of his grandparents ran through his mind. *We got to get out of this place, if it's the last thing we ever do...* He shared the verse from The Animals' rock song with his sister. He looked at Helene, who nodded. "We leave tomorrow," Tom said.

Route 78 led west, away from the inland sea. Not finding a vehicle and being impelled to walk for miles, the two arrived at the 78 intersection where they hoped to find a ride with a trucker. Antique gas-propelled trucks rusting in old barns on farm property were now the only means of moving food. These trucks were the only civilian vehicles allowed on the road. Black Sun was in the process of laying new track for destroyed or defunct rail lines and had begun to deploy antique steam engines formerly used in historic tourist rides. Trucks didn't go far because diesel fuel, in short supply, was too expensive. To deal with this situation, farmers had been forced by necessity to sell their crops at less distant locations.

The siblings succeeded in hitching a ride after Helene stood alone, blouse partly unbuttoned, with her thumb out. Only when the truck stopped did Tom show himself. The trucker pointed a shotgun at Tom, opened the door, and stepped out to make sure no one was sneaking along the side of the truck. When he saw they were unarmed, he let them approach. He wore a World Football League cap, a leather jacket, dark scarf, jeans, and construction boots. His blond hair stuck out from under the edges of the cap, and he smoked a cigar. Motioning to it, he said, "Last one I got. Can't find 'em no more. Where ya'll headed?"

Wary about revealing too much information, Helene lied. "Southwest to Reading and then to Harrisburg.

Our parents are there."

Tom was surprised at his sister's response, but, as she refused to believe their parents were dead, at least one fact in her story was true in her mind. The truck driver bought it.

"C'mon aboard." The trucker introduced himself as Lem. "Not as nice as my electric truck, but that one don't run no more. This one does. She's old but steady. I've got a small crop of corn in the back, and I'm goin' to Martinsburg, West Virginia. Ears are lean and the corn's not what it used to be. You know, they say an acre of corn eliminates eight tons of carbon dioxide from the air. I always knew we shoulda planted more corn. Now it's too late."

"We'll take a ride through to Martinsburg," Helene said.

"Thought you was goin' to Harrisburg," Lem responded.

"Yeah," she replied, thinking on her feet, "but we also got an aunt down in Winchester, Virginia and we're pretty sure she's still there. If we get off in Harrisburg and our parents aren't there, we don't want to get stuck without another ride south to find family."

"Suit yourself," Lem answered.

Tom and Helene climbed aboard. Tom sat in the front seat and Helene in the back. Lem had not specified, but it was clear that he was more comfortable with Tom next to him where he could keep an eye on him. The rough, unrepaired highway had sections where only one lane was passable due to cracks in the concrete or boulders strewn across the road. Lem said that he had often traveled that way in the old days and had just driven the road two weeks before. He knew where to detour onto side roads and how to avoid areas with a potential for ice. These days, it always looked like it would snow. One never knew.

Lem was a talker, probably because he spent so much time in his truck by himself. "Got the last of the corn crop here. Weather keeps getting worse and climate ain't no good no more. Got to go down to Georgia if a fella wants to make a living. It's warmer down there. Just like it used to be here this time of year. I still remember when we harvested in early autumn. Not much to harvest these days."

Tom spoke up after a while. "We were thinking of convincing our aunt to move down to southwest Virginia. I lived there for a while after college. Winters are cold, but at least the mountains kept the water from drowning everyone."

"Where'd you live?" Lem asked.

"Down by Blacksburg," Tom replied. "Had a job there teaching school in Christiansburg."

"Not much time for school these days," Lem responded. "People gotta survive first. Maybe someday, they'll have time for school again. The kids gotta get through the coming winter first. God, it's cold now and its only late September. What'll it be like in December?"

"Have you had any problems with people trying to steal your corn? Is the road safe from here down to Virginia?" Tom asked.

Lem was not yet sure about Tom so he gave his answer to ensure that Tom would think twice before he tried to take something. "So far I've had no problems. I've got my shotgun here. There's so little traffic on the roads and I don't usually stop for hitchhikers. If I do, I've got the shotgun and Henrietta."

Tom began twisting his head, looking around for an unseen dog, when Lem reached under his seat and brought out a loaded pistol. "Meet Henrietta. My daddy gave her to me before he passed. She's a Colt Python six shot .357 magnum and delivers a distinct punch. Had to hide her, though, when them fellas with the black uniforms stopped me. They woulda taken her. They did let me keep the shotgun for protection."

"You ran into Black Sun soldiers?" Tom asked as they entered the interchange for Route 81 south.

"I think that's what them there fellers said they were. The last time I drove north up Route 81, they had a makeshift roadblock set up just outside of Scranton. Told me if I wanted to use the road, had to pay a transportation fee. They took two boxes of corn and then put a little black flag on the back of my truck. Told me that's so I wouldn't get stopped a second time. Didn't like them fellers, but they had some firepower, so I let them take what they wanted."

"We saw them take over the town of Easton, Pennsylvania," Tom offered.

"So that's where you're coming from?" Lem asked.

"Yeah, I was picking up my sister at college to come home for the holiday when the wave hit. We got stuck there for a while."

"Family's important," Lem said.

"You have any children?" Tom asked.

"Did. Two kids and a wife as well. They was in Philadelphia visiting her sister and the in-laws when the wave hit."

"Our parents were in D.C. when the wave rolled over," Tom offered.

"Thought your parents were in Harrisburg," Lem replied.

Realizing his gaff, Tom tried to dissemble. "I meant my Mom. She was visiting D.C. Fortunately, she left a day before the surge in order to meet my Dad who was with relatives in Charlottesville. The last we heard, they both got out of Charlottesville and headed west on Route 64 but haven't heard from them since. We're not sure if they've made it back to Harrisburg." Tom was getting tied-up in his fabricated reality, so he concluded, "I think we'll go to my aunt's place in Winchester like my sister said. We know she's there."

Lem looked uneasily at Tom, but let the response slide. By that time, they had passed Harrisburg and would reach the West Virginia border before noon. The two, tired from walking, fell asleep for a while. When they woke, they were just outside Martinsburg, West Virginia. The trucker drove on.

Lem dropped them off by the roadside in the town of Martinsburg. He apologized that he couldn't take them to their "aunt's" house, but they assured him that they could make the final leg on their own. "Glad for the company," he said, though he looked relieved to be on his own again.

Once they were alone, Tom said, "Nice lie, Helene. I almost messed it up. But he got us as far as he could." He hesitated, not wanting to hurt his sister but knowing he had to ask. "You really don't believe that part about mom and dad still being alive?"

Helene closed her eyes for a second. Then she said, "Let's not talk about it."

Chapter 10
On to Harrisonburg, Virginia

Another farmer stopped for them along 81, just south of Martinsburg. He was taking a load of winter squash to Winchester. Helene waved him down, and they thanked him profusely when he dropped them near that city just off Interstate 81. There was no vehicular movement down 81, and the two walked south for what seemed like hours.

Late in the afternoon, as the sun was close to setting, they arrived at an abandoned rest stop. It was a brick and cement building with parking spaces for cars in front, truckers in the rear, bathrooms, and a tourist info area in the middle. A separate annex for vending machines stood next to the main building. The place had not seen a visitor in weeks. There were no vehicles in front. The machines in the annex were empty, and broken glass littered the floor. However, in a private office at the back of the administration building, a machine had been overlooked. Tom smashed the glass and removed candy bars and packets of chips.

They now had enough food to last them for a couple of days, if they were careful.

The toilets were not functional, but they used them anyway. The sinks also had no running water. After exploring the area to see what was upstream, they washed their faces and upper bodies in a nearby stream where the ice-cold water burned their skin. Certain that there was no danger from animal runoff or hazardous chemicals that may have spilled in the area, they captured water that ran over a series of rocks and drank their fill. The two ate some chips and waited in the fading sun, hoping someone might stop. Wanting to travel further south before nightfall, Tom and Helene began to walk the short distance back to Route 81.

As the siblings walked back under a fading sun, two soldiers in Black Sun uniforms stepped in front of them. "Stay calm," Tom said. "Just remember our story."

Helene, thinking of Easton, involuntarily shuddered but willed herself to be calm. The soldiers asked for ID and both Tom and Helene showed Virginia driver licenses. The siblings had kept them for psychological reasons; a way of clinging to what seemed familiar, sane, and not apocalyptic.

That part went well, but when the soldiers asked where they were going, Tom needed to invent a better story than the one he had told Lem. He quickly settled on: "I work and live in Blacksburg, but we were visiting outside of D.C. when the wave hit. We were on high ground and hitched a ride to Winchester, Virginia, but it wasn't good there. We decided to go to Blacksburg, where I still have friends, and figured the best way was down 81."

The taller soldier with bars on his shoulder and a holstered pistol answered, "You're probably right. Our convoy's headed to Harrisonburg, Virginia, and we can give you a lift if our commander agrees. Just stopped here for water." As he finished speaking, a voice came over the radio.

"Good to go?"

The taller soldier responded. "A-okay, Commander. Come on in." Within minutes, another jeep and four trucks full of troops pulled into the rest stop.

A short, stocky soldier without the bars mentioned off-handedly, "We're A Division, Brigade B, Battalion C, Black Sun Army out of Pittsburgh." When Tom stared at him with a blank look, the soldier said, "Don't you know anything? A Black Sun division has 10,000 men, a Brigade 3,500 men and our battalion around 1,000. We got four platoons here with us, fifty men each."

The taller soldier quickly intervened. "Shut your mouth, Jim. Can't be given' our numbers out to strangers. Maybe they're spies."

Jim replied, "Didn't mean no harm, lieutenant, they seem okay."

Tom interjected. "There's no water here. You can get water in the creek over there." He pointed to the creek where they had washed. "No electricity either. Look, we just gotta get to Blacksburg." Tom felt that staying with the truth was his best option. "We don't care about what you're doing, just so that you can get us closer to Blacksburg and my apartment."

"Let me talk to the commander," the lieutenant responded.

He saluted as the commander stepped from the second jeep and began issuing orders. "These two want a ride to Harrisonburg, sir. There's a creek over there where we can fill all the canteens and water barrels."

The commander issued a swift order. "Make it fast. Check for runoff from hazardous sources first. We'll push through to Harrisonburg. It's only seventy miles away. Doesn't look like there are any major obstacles according to the report I received. A helicopter flew over the road a few days ago." He then proceeded with an impatient stride toward the bathrooms, leaving Tom and Helene with the two soldiers.

The soldiers also stepped inside the building. When they came back, the commander had returned to his jeep and motioned for the four trucks to move forward. "You can take those two if you want," he said, motioning to Tom and Helene.

Tom sat in silence. The lieutenant and Helene seemed to hit it off right away. He seemed to fancy her. He came from a small town in the Poconos near Easton, where Helene had been at school. They both loved skiing and had visited the same ski resorts. The conversation seemed to evoke fond memories for the officer of another time, another life. During the drive to Harrisonburg, it took both their minds off the new post-surge reality.

Although the road was choppy, there were no major problems, and they entered Harrisonburg just as night fell. The town now looked like a fortified camp. Black Sun had zoned off a rectangular area, the "protected zone," that included James Madison University and Route 81 that cut through the center of the rectangle. The JMU campus dominated most of the west side, and the JMU Convention Center and housing areas sat to the east of Route 81.

Tom had visited a high school friend at JMU years before and, although the physical layout remained the same, the place no longer resembled a college campus. Barbed wire surrounded the "protected zone" and roadblocks were set up at check points at all entrances/exits to the zone. The Brigade Headquarters was located at the former JMU Convocation Center, and a makeshift airfield sat west of 81 on the campus main quad. Several helicopters sat on the grass. A squad of soldiers defended the camp's main water supply, Newman Lake.

After the convoy turned off Route 81 at the Harrisonburg exit, it dropped one platoon at the airfield to reinforce those protecting the helicopters and left the main contingent of soldiers at several JMU dorms converted to barracks. Then the trucks and the jeep carrying Tom and Helene pulled up to the military supply center at Bridgeforth Stadium. The commander's jeep drove on ahead to report to Brigade Headquarters.

As Tom and Helene got out of the jeep, the lieutenant commented, "Look miss, you guys need to stay inside the protected zone. If you exit past the checkpoints, they won't let you in again. I'm going to give you a zone pass, which is good for one night. I am also going to write a short note. It says that you are authorized to continue south using Black Sun military transport. The pass is good for tonight and the travel order is good for tomorrow. Be back here at the stadium early tomorrow morning. Show this to the gate guard, and he'll find you transportation to Roanoke. Our troops are moving south to reinforce a new base there."

The lieutenant and his companion drove through the gate, leaving Helene and Tom standing alone at the entrance. With night falling, they were not sure of what to do. The siblings began walking west along University Avenue, hoping to find an abandoned building where they could stay. Trying to stay at the campus dorms, now barracks, was out of the question. The streets had no functioning streetlights, and they walked by the light of the almost full moon. With only the celestial orb to light their way, they moved slightly north, making sure not to go past a roadblock. Before reaching the northern exit out of the zone, they found an abandoned Fairfield Inn hotel.

The double glass doors to the lobby were locked, but Tom had an idea. "Do you have a pen?" he asked.

Helene rummaged through her backpack and pulled one out. "Like this?"

He nodded and took the pen, then scoured the area for a rock. Lifting a medium sized rock he found on what was left of the walkway, he approached the doors.

"What are you doing?" Helene asked.

"Something I learned from Dad a long time ago." Aiming the pen at the bottom portion of the door hinge, he added, "Be ready to remove the pin if I can knock it out. I just hope this pen doesn't break." He tapped the bottom of the pen with the rock, and after a few minutes, the pin on the hinge lifted. "Grab it," he ordered, and Helene pulled the pin out. They repeated the exercise, and after a while, removed the pins.

"But it's still locked," Helene said. "How are we going to open it?"

"We're taking the pins off the other door, too. Then we'll remove both at the same time."

Helene had doubts, but in the end, it worked. Both doors were removed.

It had gotten quite cold as they entered the lobby. Tom located some old brochures and papers, which he rolled up and surrounded with twigs he found outside the hotel. He then lit the papers inside the triangle. As the fire grew, he put on more twigs and crumpled paper and fed the flames with a broken wooden chair. Leftover chips and candy became their dinner. They took two busted sofas and pushed them close to the fire. Although worried about soldiers, they had a permit and, exhausted from the day's activities, they quickly fell asleep.

Chapter 11
The Road to Roanoke

The next morning, after a breakfast of stale chips and dated candy, the siblings walked back through the cold streets. As usual, the sky was covered in a cloudy haze. The weakened sun had not yet begun to shine. The weather mirrored their state of mind. Would they find the ride they needed? When they arrived at the stadium, Tom presented the lieutenant's note to the guard and mentioned they had been told they could hitch a ride to Roanoke. "Are you sure we can trust them?" Helene asked.

"What choice do we have," Tom replied.

Within two hours, they climbed aboard a truck carrying supplies to that city.

The weather remained cold and the heated truck cabin had room for only four, so the siblings huddled in the back of the unheated, tarp-covered transport vehicle. About an hour outside of Harrisonburg, the truck stopped at an abandoned rest stop. Tom and Helene both jumped out. "We need a bathroom break," Helene told the soldiers.

Looking at Helene, Tom whispered,"Will you be okay by yourself? Do you want me to go with you?"

"I don't know how much time they'll give us. It will be faster if you go for the food. I'll watch my back. I'll yell if I need you."

Tom told the soldier who seemed to be in charge, "I'm going to check for food, if that's okay?"

With the soldier's permission, Tom ran to the machine hut while Helene looked for the women's bathroom. When Tom left, the four soldiers were milling about, checking their truck. As he reached the vending machine area, Tom saw two soldiers heading for the men's toilets. One of them, a tall, aggressive-looking man, had a pistol and a knife at his side. With his gait and manner, he looked like someone who would dare the world to fight him. Another soldier, thin and sickly looking with a small pencil moustache, bad teeth, and a sorrowful smile, followed.

Tom didn't find any food during his quick search, and

when he returned to the truck, Helene was not there. She had not called him, so he began to worry. The two soldiers who had gone in the direction of the toilets stood by the truck, laughing. One was zipping his pants. The other cleaned a knife on his pants leg. A cold chill ran through him. He panicked and ran in the direction of the women's toilets. "Helene," he yelled. "Helene, where are you?"

Helene appeared in the doorway, hair tangled, blood on her lips, shirt torn, and one breast uncovered. Although she was trying to zip her jeans, her hand trembled so much she was unable to complete the task. As Tom reached her, Helene lowered her eyes and stared at the ground. Her body shook with silent sobs, and she appeared to have lost her voice.

He quickly pulled her to him. "For God's sake, Helene, what happened?" he yelled. "Did they hurt you? I'll kill them!" He released her for a second and punched the wall until his knuckles bloodied. It took him a moment to realize it was not about him. His sister could quickly go into shock.

Drawing on some internal strength, Helene found enough voice to whisper between her clenched teeth, "Don't do anything. They'll kill you! Just let it be."

As Tom reached out again, she almost fell into his arms. "Let me help with the jeans." Blood was splattered on her jeans and socks. "Are you okay?" he sobbed. "Are you okay?"

Helene's body continued to tremble, and she could not look Tom in the eyes. Tears silently dripped down her cheeks, forming a wet spot at the torn collar and neckline. She gasped, as if she could not get enough air.

"I tried to fight, I really did, but they put a knife to my throat, then cut me… down there." She pointed to her groin area. "They…" She tried to steady her breath. "They said they were going to kill me, and they laughed about it." She covered her face with her hands. "I really tried to stop them… I really did."

"Helene." Tom's voice trembled with mounting anger. "Don't think about it. You did what you had to. Are you still bleeding?"

"I tried to use my… my rags. The ones for my period. I tried to use that and cold water to stop the blood." The tears covered her face now and snot dribbled down from her nose. "It wasn't my first time. I mean, I've had a boyfriend, but it was not like that. They were rough, and it hurts. It hurts… inside."

"When we get to Roanoke, we need to find a doctor,"

Tom said gently as he helped her walk back to the truck.

"Tom," she whispered, "Don't say anything. They told me if I said anything, they'd say we were spies and shoot us. They could shoot us now."

"If I get the chance…" he said. But Tom had no weapon and no opportunity, so he didn't finish the sentence. When they returned to the truck, Tom glared at the two soldiers. The tall blond un-holstered his gun and waited. When Tom did nothing, the two turned their backs on him and continued to laugh. As the truck left the rest stop, hail began to fall and a cold rain followed them. Helene had her head on Tom's shoulder all the way to Roanoke. She said nothing, but her body continued to convulse.

Arriving in Roanoke, the truck drove straight to the airport where Black Sun had established a military base. From the Roanoke airport, the Black Sun soldiers were able to observe the mountains on both sides. To the east were the Blue Ridge and Mill Mountain and to the west the Alleghenies. Tom remembered the time during college when he visited the area and had seen a neon-lit star that shone after dark atop Mill Mountain. With no electricity, he assumed the mountain would now remain in darkness.

Tom helped his sister climb down from the truck. She still appeared to be in pain and winced as she put her foot on the ground. The two began to walk away, but they had gotten only a few yards when two soldiers approached them. The soldiers blocked their progress. One said, "Black Sun Military Security. We've been informed that the two of you are suspected spies and are trying to discover our strength here in Roanoke. We need to ask you some questions. Come with us." The two soldiers led them to an old corrugated steel airplane hangar.

Tom realized that the soldiers from the truck wanted to make sure that he and Helene never got a chance to tell their story, at least not to anyone who would believe them.

Tom put his arm around his sister. "We'll get through this," he whispered.

Chapter 12
Cross and Crescent

As the door to the cell closed behind him with a loud clink, Tom wondered where they had put Helene. An officer had told them, "We are separating the two of you and will compare your stories. If you're lying, we'll shoot you both."

Tom sat in silence for about an hour before they came for him. He had too much time to consider his fate. He had told his sister they would get through this, but he was not so sure. There did not seem to be a way out. Two soldiers dragged him to another room, shoved him in a chair, and tied his wrists to the chair's arms. A tall, tubercular-looking officer with lumps on his neck, face hard and pockmarked, puffed on a cigarette as he approached. He was coughing and wheezing, and his putrid breath smelled like death. Without hesitation, he jammed the point of the lit cigarette into Tom's arm and hissed, "Have I got your full attention?" Tom felt the flame burn into his flesh and tried to block out the danger signals from his nerve endings.

Like a cobra before a strike, the officer's head weaved from side to side as he sized up his prey. Then came the first question. "Who are you spying for, and what is your mission?"

Despite the pain, Tom tried to focus and keep his voice level. "My sister and I were trying to find our parents in Harrisburg, Pennsylvania. We couldn't find them, so now we're on our way to join friends in Blacksburg. That's all, I'm no spy." He hoped Helene was giving the same story.

The translucent-skinned officer slid to the back of Tom's chair and hovered over his neck like a hungry vampire. His breath felt warm on Tom's neck. "You're talking about friends in the Free City of Blacksburg? Did you know Blacksburg has sent out a radio message asking us not to visit them? Soon, we will be forced to pay them a visit. Now, tell me about your friends!"

The officer did not like Tom's answer. Tom sat and stared straight ahead, wondering what the officer was doing. Out of nowhere, a hammer-like object came down hard on one of Tom's fingers, again and again. Tom screamed in pain, unable to stop the assault. As Tom screamed, the officer asked another question. "What do you know about this Cross and Crescent?"

Choking on the pain, Tom whispered he knew nothing. The wraith of a man seemed to enjoy taking a slow drag on his cigarette and putting it daintily in an ashtray before carefully retrieving the hammer he had left on the table. He proceeded to break another finger. This time, Tom fainted.

Tom woke up alone in his cell. He was surprised when the guards opened his cell door and threw Helene inside. "Are you okay?" he asked her. "Are you in pain?"

"No," Helene whispered. "They slapped me in the face a few times and then pulled off my clothes. When they saw the cut, the swelling, and dried blood, they figured out that someone had preceded them. I asked for a doctor and they promised they would send one if I told them the truth."

Again, her body shook, and Tom wondered how much more his sister could take. Speaking even more softly, she continued, "I only told them what we agreed on. We were looking for our parents and then decided to go to

Blacksburg, where you lived and worked. I don't know if they believed me, but they gave me an hour to decide on my answer and let me know getting a doctor depended on a truthful response. The next thing, they gave me my clothes back and dragged me through the corridors and I ended up here in your cell."

When Tom got up to hug her, his right hand hung limply by his side. Helene gasped at the sight of his swollen, crooked fingers. "Oh, what have they done to you?" She sobbed. "We could die here." As Tom sat down again, Helene turned around in despair. Taking her eyes off him, she noticed the cell had a window facing the mountain.

Trying to get her mind off what would probably happen to them, Tom told her, "Look out the window and tell me what you see."

Just then, darkness fell and a brilliant light appeared atop Mill Mountain. "The mountain, it's lit," she said.

Tom slowly raised himself, holding his broken-fingered hand with the other, and unsteadily moved to the window. "That's not the star," he said. "What is that?"

"It's a crescent with a cross superimposed over it. A cross and a crescent. That's what it is," Helene replied. "It's lighting up the whole top of the mountain, brighter than any Christmas star."

Tom mused aloud, "I wonder how they got that lit? Perhaps a generator? Someone is up there."

A commotion from the hallway pulled their attention back. Gun shots sounded, and five masked men appeared in front of the cell door.

The apparent leader, a thick growth of beard evident under his ski mask, carried a Glock and had a large knife attached to his belt. He asked the man behind him, "Do you have the keys?"

The man directly behind passed him a set of keys. "Here you go." This tall, lanky fellow and his comrades carried automatic weapons with replacement clips in pouches attached to their belts.

"We need to let all the prisoners out," the leader ordered. "We can recruit these people later. We don't have much time before more guards arrive. We can't hold this location for long. They weren't expecting such a foolhardy move. We surprised them."

The leader opened the cell door. "Let's move," he said, and motioned with his gun for Tom and Helene to follow. They moved from room to room, opening cell doors and stepping over dead Black Sun soldiers lying in the various positions where they had fallen. Other dead bodies slumped over desks. Within moments, the siblings and twenty now-released prisoners were ushered through a series of corridors to a truck waiting outside. They climbed into the back.

Tom addressed the leader. "My sister needs medical attention. She was raped."

"The bastards will pay. We've got a medic who can see to her when we get to camp at the mountain top."

Chapter 13
Mill Mountain

Only one road ascended to the top of Mill Mountain. This winding road led through a pine forest, past old abandoned homes, and dead-ended in a parking lot cul-de-sac located in front of a former petting zoo at the trailhead of a nature park. The place was easy to defend as the road had so many cutbacks and, although the mountain was treeless on top, the pine trees farther down protected the rebels from anything moving overhead. A small group of men hidden among the rocks and trees could easily ambush any column or vehicle moving up the mountain road.

As they entered the old park ranger's office, one of the women who greeted the newly released prisoners took charge of Helene and led her to a makeshift infirmary. "Don't worry," she told Tom as she ushered Helene out of the room. "I'll take good care of her."

Another fighter brought Tom and some of the other former prisoners to a room furnished with a picnic table and chairs. When they entered, they saluted the apparent leader, a short man who wore just a hunting jacket and no uniform. While a medic cleaned, splinted, and bandaged his fingers, Tom looked around the room. A topographical map of Virginia stretched across the table. Since there were no cell towers and no signals due to problems with satellites, and with online maps gone, everyone had to rely on old-fashioned maps. Someone had marked an East Coast-Middle Atlantic map showing Black Sun bases with red pins and placed it on a wall. One pin for each Black Sun base. Tom could see those in Pennsylvania, Maryland, and Virginia. Harrisonburg didn't have a pin.

Looking at the apparent leader, Tom said, "You'd better put a pin on Harrisonburg. There's a substantial presence there, and they are preparing to move south to Blacksburg after they finish here."

The short man looked like an average senior citizen. With a receding hairline and his remaining black hair slicked back, he might have been an early-bird customer at the famous retiree watering hole, *The Golden Years Corral*. He looked at Tom with interest. "How do you know that?" he said, obviously intrigued. "By the way, you can call me Stephens."

"Because we talked to some of their soldiers on the way to Harrisonburg and saw a base with an airport and helicopters, a football stadium full of trucks and armored vehicles, and a large headquarters. The son of a bitch who broke my fingers told me Blacksburg was next on the list. He was interested in you guys. He mentioned a Cross and Crescent. I saw it light up on this mountain. Are you guys the Cross and Crescent?"

The short man paused, thought a moment, and then responded, "We are part of a world movement called the Cross and Crescent dedicated to religious freedom for all and tolerance of all races, sexes, and creeds. Blacksburg has some of our comrades who formed a 'Free City' and are putting together a defense. We don't know the details because contact with them has been almost impossible. Black Sun has been jamming our communications. What else do you know?"

"That's all," Tom said. "But I would like to hear more about you… about Cross and Crescent."

"We don't know much here, because we're still getting everything together," Stephens replied. "We just got the word that there was a resistance to Black Sun here in the United States. There have been sporadic shortwave radio reports, and we believe there may be similar organizations that have taken over in other countries. We've organized under the Cross and Crescent banner and so has Blacksburg. Some say that the movement's world headquarters is in Brasilia, Brazil. Don't know that for a fact."

Stephens turned and started pacing. "The word is that way up on a high plateau, the former Brazilian capital has attracted a group of New Age thinkers. They are working on a plan to reverse the coming Ice Age. I don't know if I believe it. People say that these New Age thinkers believe that the world's problems stem from polluted thoughts of greed, hatred, and selfish concerns for material things. If polluted thinking brings a polluted world, then we can logically deduce that purifying thought will purify the world. The world is just an objective manifestation of our thoughts; kind of like an old film projector transmits images to a screen."

"It sounds awfully esoteric and metaphysical," Tom replied. "I've read about such theories when I took philosophy in college." Then Tom remembered Easton's Bunker Hill, visualizing the very moment the Humvee's gun cut the small band of resisters on the hill to pieces. The sky had turned red, then black, and then the golf ball sized hail rained down. There were small tornados. It would be strange if there were some connection between emotion and weather. He considered the idea, but thought, *That would be just too weird.*

"Where were you headed when they arrested you?" Stephens asked.

"Blacksburg," Tom answered. "I live there and used to work in Christiansburg."

"So you know Route 11?" Stephens asked.

"Sure do. Before all this, I used to take Route 81 north toward Waynesboro and then on to Richmond. Sometimes, to avoid congestion, I would take Route 11 to the West of 81 through the mountains. Why do you ask?"

"I need someone to take a message to Blacksburg. It's written in code and summarizes what we know about Black Sun's plans and intentions, as well as their force here in Roanoke. We've been fighting them for several weeks now and have a feel for what they can do. The Free City of Blacksburg will need all the info we can provide if, as you say, the Roanoke Black Sun garrison is getting ready to march on them."

"Do they have a defense?" Tom asked.

"Yes, they are building a militia and have some equipment. I can give you a motorcycle and an extra can of gas if you'll warn them. Will you go? You've got to leave early tomorrow morning. We are expecting an assault, and if they have helicopters, we're pretty open here on the mountain. We can fend off the Humvees and tanks on the winding road but eventually… We can buy some time, but we can't afford to send anyone here to help Blacksburg."

"I'll go," Tom said. "But I want my sister to come with me. I can't leave her here, even if there is no attack. If they do attack, she will need to get out too."

"You can take her if she's medically fit," the short man said. "I'll get someone to find you a motorcycle. You can ride, I suppose?"

"I've ridden small bikes, but I'll take one of those old Harleys I saw in your motor pool. It'll be better for the two of us. It'll eat more gas but on these mountain roads it can stand up to a rough ride."

"Okay. We'll find your sister and get you both a place to sleep. At five tomorrow morning, meet me back here."

Stephens had some of his men give Tom and Helene some sleeping bags and a mat to sleep on. Helene had been cleared to travel. They were awakened at five the next morning, and a soldier took them to meet Stephens. As they walked to the command building, the sound of *The Star-Spangled Banner* filled the air. A soldier was raising the "Stars and Stripes" along with a flag showing a cross that was imposed over a crescent. The words *by the dawn's early light* filled Tom's thoughts.

As promised, Stephens provided food, an old red, gas-fueled Harley 500XZ, and a spare canister filled with gasoline. Stephens told Tom, "She's a six-speed, weighs only 395 pounds, built of graphite and steel alloy, sits real low, has a low center of gravity and takes four gallons in the tank; a dual on/off road bike that will do well in the mountains."

They left before Black Sun could block the road off the mountain. Creeping through Roanoke's back streets, they reached Route 81 and then found a way across it by going cross-country and picking up Route 11. From the hilltops to the west of 81, they looked down on the city of Roanoke. It looked like ants were moving toward Mill Mountain, holding what appeared to be small sticks in front. At that moment, one of the sticks flashed, and crimson spots dotted the side of Mill Mountain. The tanks were doing major damage. As they watched, small hornet-like things moved through the air toward the hilltop. *Helicopters*, Tom thought. A rumbling of thunder echoed in the distance, and black storm clouds hovered over Mill Mountain. Then the road turned, and they were out of view of the valley. He wondered if the Cross and Crescent would still be lit over Mill Mountain that evening.

Chapter 14

On to Blacksburg

The lioness moved silently over the rocky terrain. She was solid gold with black whiskers under her nose. Her eyes were dark, and her teeth and claws were razor sharp. She was hungry. Since she had left the zoo near Pittsburg, she had eaten little. The cat had migrated a long distance and had traversed mostly mountains and forest and avoided human settlements. The cold had sent the deer population farther southwest, and rabbits and squirrels were not enough to keep a lioness alive. As she sat on the overhanging cliff just above the deserted Route 11, she heard a new sound. The source of the sound was approaching. It wasn't a deer but something different.

The siblings had just rounded a mountain turn and reached the top of an overlook located below an overhanging cliff. Tom slowed the engine to five miles an hour so they could look out over the valley below. The cat didn't hesitate. As they passed under her, the cat leaped from its perch and landed in the middle of the road. Tom quickly swerved to avoid her.

Tom and Helene were thrown off the motorcycle, and Helene hit her head and lay unconscious on the road. Tom rolled to his feet and turned to face the cat, who was beginning a traditional mock attack from the rear. As Tom turned, the cat stopped and then charged again. Hungry, she wanted to sink her teeth into Tom's exposed neck and then break his spine. It was only a moment, but it was enough time for Tom to bring his helmet between himself and the cat's jaws. He swung at the cat and hit her in the face, temporarily stopping her advance but falling backward in the process. He quickly drew his knife and swiped at the animal as he rolled backward towards the motorcycle. His leather jacket spared him any damage to his arms, and he held his helmet by the visor and used it to protect his face from the animal's claws. He continued to jab at the cat, who backed off and prepared for a third attack. Tom leapt to the overturned bike, grabbed his loaded shotgun from the carrying case and fired as the cat launched herself through the air. Projectiles from both barrels struck the cat in mid-air. The animal fell dead at Tom's feet. To make sure, Tom quickly reloaded and shot the cat in the head. He felt bad about killing the animal, but in this strange new world, survival was everything.

As Tom moved to where Helene lay, she began to stir. "Look at me. Do you know who I am? Do you know where you are?"

"I'm just a bit groggy," she replied, sitting up. "And I have a hell of a headache, but I think the helmet protected my head from damage. I don't feel woozy or dizzy, and I'm not disoriented."

Tom replied, "That's my sister. Always the scientific one. Only you could self-diagnose with such ease. We'll have to be careful from now on. I think you'd better keep your pistol close as we move forward." Tom righted the bike, which had suffered minimal damage. However, he quickly observed that when the bike fell, the spare gasoline canister was broken and their extra gas was forming a pool on the poorly paved road.

"I hope we still have enough gas left to make the outskirts of Christiansburg," Helene said, with wrinkles quickly forming on her brow.

Tom kept one eye on the road and the other on the gas gauge. As the minutes ticked by, the gauge dropped, and Tom's body tensed. His fingers were white as he clutched the handlebars in frustration and desperation. Two hours after the cat attack, the bike's motor began to sputter and finally died from lack of petrol. A sign on the side of the road read *Christiansburg six miles*. "We'll have to push the bike from here." Tom said. "If we can find some gas, we can make it to Blacksburg."

There was no one on the road to stop and help. Their arms ached from pushing the heavy bike up the hills. At least they could coast when the road went down the mountain. Keeping the key in the ignition enabled them to leave the bike in neutral, but controlling it coasting down the winding road was not easy. They almost went off the side of the mountain on several occasions. The cat attack had happened around noon. It was dark when they completed the six miles to Christiansburg.

Car dealerships, vehicle-charging stations, and a few antique gas stations lined the entrance to Christiansburg as Route 11 approached the Route 81 exit. The charging stations were abandoned and eerily quiet during what was formerly evening rush hour. After searching several locations, the two located an old gas station where the owner admitted he had some gasoline. "Pumps don't work, no electricity," said the grizzled owner. "But I got a gas-run generator and pumped some earlier, so I got some cans of gas in the back. You're welcome to take what you need. That bike don't take much, and I can spare a few gallons." The next eight miles by bike to Blacksburg seemed like heaven after the six they had walked.

Chapter 15
The Free City of Blacksburg

As their Harley roared out of Christiansburg, Tom and Helene discovered Route 460 ended abruptly at the Blacksburg border. The short bridge to Blacksburg was gone, and this was clearly not the result of changing climate. Someone had deliberately blown it to prevent vehicles from moving forward. The two proceeded off-road until they reached the other side of the gulley where they were forced to stop at a blockade on 460. Positioned at the Blacksburg side of the missing bridge, four middle-aged soldiers wearing fatigues and green berets manned the blockade.

"State your business," barked the officer in charge.

"Why do you want to enter the Free City of Blacksburg?"

"I'm Tom Rogers and this is my sister, Helene Rogers. Here's our driver's licenses," Tom said, handling them to the officer. "You can see it's us in the pictures. We have an important message for whomever is in command." Tom passed the soldier the encrypted message the short man in Roanoke had given him. As he handed the document to the soldier, he noticed a wax seal that had somehow escaped his attention.

"I recognize the seal," said the officer. "Get them in a jeep. Henry, drive them to Commander Wilson. This is definitely from the resistance at Roanoke."

The two were whisked away in an old army jeep. Henry, the young driver, apparently enjoyed his job, as he was laughing with glee while taking turns on two wheels. Due to his prowess at the wheel, or perhaps his lack of concern for his own life or the lives of others, they arrived at the Virginia Tech campus in less than ten minutes. The Blacksburg Militia headquarters was located in Burruss Hall, a former admissions building.

Tom couldn't help but dwell on how much change had occurred at Virginia Tech since he had been there just weeks before. That July, he had taught a summer-session evening course in history at the campus to supplement his income from his high school teaching job. With sadness, he remembered the groups of co-eds strolling casually across the drill field as they walked to class on lazy and soft summer Blacksburg nights. Now, snow was everywhere, the co-eds were gone, and the entire campus had the feel of a military base on high alert.

Someone must have radioed ahead as a tall, muscular soldier wearing fatigues met them on the steps of Burruss Hall. His jacket was adorned with a shoulder patch that illustrated a dagger going through a lightning bolt, and he wore a green beret. A holstered Glock 19 pistol was attached to the belt at his side. "I'm Sergeant Major Easter, and I'll take you to Commander Wilson," he said.

As they followed the sergeant up the steps and into the building, the two noticed he walked with a marked limp and had the bearing of a professional military man. However, there were things about him that did not match Tom's image of a typical professional soldier. His red hair was longer than a soldier's would be and his mustache and the scraggly beard on his chin and cheeks had not been trimmed.

When they reached the second floor, the sergeant ushered them down a long hall toward a closed door. He knocked and called out, "Commander Wilson?"

"Enter," a strong, gruff voice responded from inside. The sergeant opened the door, and the siblings saw a middle-aged man with graying hair sitting behind a desk and examining road maps. From behind glasses, his blue eyes sized them up. His crisp pressed uniform hinted at a will that would not bend.

"Sir, I've brought the two who arrived at the checkpoint with a message from Roanoke."

"Thank you, Josh," the Commander said. "I want you to stay while I read this. Please sit down."

"Very good, Sir," replied the Sergeant, who then placed himself in a chair to the right of the Commander.

Turning to Tom and Helene, he said, "Please sit down, you two. You look like you've had a hard journey." Tom handed him the document. After breaking the seal, the commander scanned it with intense concentration. "It says here that you two have information on the massing of enemy forces in Harrisonburg and their intent to reinforce Roanoke before launching an attack on this city. It also says the resistance rescued you from a Black Sun prison. By the way, how is Roanoke doing? I understand that they are holed-up at a base on top of Mill Mountain, but we haven't heard from them for several weeks."

"That's because Black Sun has been blocking all

communications out of Roanoke," Tom replied. "That's why they sent us. Things did not look good when we left. As we hit Route 81 on our way south, we saw the beginning of an assault on Mill Mountain. Tanks were firing from below and helicopters from above. They knew there was no hope of help, but I know they won't yield until there is no one left to fight."

"Sir," the Sergeant quickly spoke up. "I'd like to take some men and go to their aid. A buddy of mine, Staff Sergeant Horrowitz, is there. We spent time in the sand box before rescuing those Americans in the Dom Rep and Costa Rica. You remember when things went bad in 2040 and the local governments expropriated their property and held them hostage? We got them all out without losing a man. We take care of our own and don't leave men behind."

"I know your code," the Commander replied, "but it would be a suicide mission, and I can't afford to lose you. Not now. We've got to be ready when they come."

"At least we could ambush them along 81 and slow them down a bit."

"Josh, with the small amount of trained men here, we've got to pick our battles. They intend to wipe us out. They won't leave an island of resistance behind them as they move to control the whole east coast. If they get past us, they will take Asheville next, then Charlotte and then Atlanta if they haven't already moved on them from their Texas base. With Charleston and Savanah under water, shipping is being done out of Charlotte and Atlanta-Macon." The commander shook his head. "We need to buy time for the Cross and Crescent group forming in Latin America. The farther Black Sun moves south, the closer they come to building a jump-off site from which to launch a fleet toward South or Central America."

"Are you guys Cross and Crescent?" Tom inquired. "The Commander at Mill Mountain said that only that group's resistance could defeat Black Sun. Is all that esoteric stuff true?"

"Look, son, I'd love to discuss Cross and Crescent theology with you, but we just ain't got time. Our job is to buy time for those people in Brasilia so they can get the world back together. I'm sorry about Stephens, though. You know he was a Virginia senator in a previous government, the one before the last government overthrown by Black Sun. A real people person. He rallied the resistance in Roanoke. The way he could motivate men… It doesn't sound like he made it out. We've lost a good leader and a patriot."

Wiping the corner of his eyes with the back of his hand, the Commander continued, "Sergeant Easter, take charge of these two and debrief them on any further details, anything they may know or have seen. Oh, and, Josh, I know you would never leave a brother behind. But don't think of going AWOL on me. We need you here. Dismissed."

He returned to studying his maps, but seemed not to focus on them as his eyes wandered to a photo on the wall. It was a picture of a group of men in suits lined up in front of what looked like the former U.S. Capitol.

Is the now-deceased Stephens among them? Tom wondered.

The meeting finished, the siblings and Josh walked across the drill field to where the old Student Center stood. The Blacksburg Militia had turned the building into a mess hall. "You guys look hungry," Josh said. "Let's get some hot soup into you." Once inside the building, Josh began his debrief.

Tom summarized their experiences, starting with Easton, then Harrisonburg, and finally Roanoke. When he finished, Josh had more questions.

"So tell me more about the makeshift airfield in Harrisonburg and those helicopters. Do you remember what the helicopters looked like?"

Tom proceeded to describe what he had seen before they went to the Stadium.

Josh continued, "It sounds to me like they have Blackhawk and Chinook transport helicopters and the newer UH 1000 Apache attack helicopters equipped with the old Hellfire missiles and new Sparrow missiles as well as the latest laser turret guns. That's the best the old Army had that could be run without computers. All the computer run equipment is useless now."

When Tom described the vehicles and tanks he had seen, the sergeant knit his brows, rubbed his forehead and said, "Those sound like non-electric/non-solar Humvees and all-purpose vehicles and the 2070 Viper tanks equipped with both traditional and laser weaponry. I wonder how they got the tanks running. Without the computers, they may have jerry-rigged some battery-operated control equipment. We have nothing that will match that.

"We have a 2020 Abrams battle tank made by General Dynamics with the old Honeywell turbine engine. It's equipped with a heavy machine gun. We had to do a work-around on the guidance system. The Virginia National Guard did not go over to Black Sun.

The closest unit in Danville grabbed the Abrams from the Tank Museum on the North Carolina border. We tested it last week and it works, but we have a limited number of shells and ammo. They also brought a 2020 antique Raytheon Stinger FIM-92F surface-to-air, man-portable missile. It's equipped with an infrared seeker, called the old 'fire and forget'. It can hit a target at 15,000 feet, if not identified and destroyed by an airship's defense systems. I tested it last week. Hated to waste one of the six missiles, but we've got five left.

"The old mortars the guard brought with them are still functional, but we don't have much ammunition. They also brought two gas-operated Cougar light tactical vehicles and two ancient Humvees that were in the Armory, as well as some shotguns, rifles, and light and medium machine guns. All of them are functional, but we're short on ammunition. The guard got out just before the sea rushed in and flowed all the way to the Blue Ridge. What we have won't be much against helicopters and tanks, especially if the choppers drop men behind our lines near the mountains to the west."

Tom spoke up. "If Black Sun brings troops from both Harrisonburg and Roanoke, that could mean a one-thousand-man battalion or a brigade of 3,500 troops. Do you have enough men to stop them?"

Josh knit his brows again. "We've got thirty National Guard troops and about sixty volunteers, some with former military experience, like myself. There are also fifty ROTC students from Virginia Tech. That makes a hundred and forty in all. The cadets are young, but this will not be the first time cadets have had to fight.

Josh took a breath and continued, "I think that's enough for today. Let's find you guys a place to sleep. There are plenty of dormitory rooms, but none have heat. We have blankets, though." He led them to a vacant stone and brick dormitory across the quad from the old student center. They walked slowly, following the limping Sergeant Christmas across the snow-covered campus. After they entered the building and climbed the stairs to the second floor, he asked, "Do you guys mind sleeping in the same room?"

"No problem. We'd rather remain together," Helene said, still focused on the incident on route 81.

When he left them, Josh said, "Tomorrow, I'll meet you in front of Burruss Hall and take you to breakfast. Oh, and by the way, they brought your Harley up here. It's parked in front of the former admin building. You can pick it up tomorrow."

After a troubled night's sleep under a mound of blankets in a cold dorm room, the two walked to Burruss Hall to meet Sergeant Easter. He drove them to a local breakfast/coffee shop, La Petite Café Crème. The place had been a popular restaurant back in the day, but for the last year, it served only French coffee, croissants, *croque monsieurs*, omelets, and quiche. The owner, Antoine Lemaire, a Franco-American dual citizen, was originally from New York. When Josh entered, Antoine gave him a big hug and a kiss on both cheeks. "Mon amie, ça fait trop du temps. Qu'est-ce que tu deviens?"

Josh replied, "Très occupé. Been busy preparing a surprise party for our Black Sun neighbors in Roanoke. They may be on their way here soon. Let me introduce my two young friends, Tom and Helene."

"Enchanté. Mais qu'elle est belle! Avec un nom français. Elene."

"I know some French," Tom said to his sister. "It appears he likes you, Helene." He directed his next words at Josh. "Does he always speak French?"

"Non," Antoine said. "But after all the time in La Legion and now running a French restaurant, il faut parler Français."

"So Josh," Tom queried. "Where did you learn French?"

Josh's answer was short. "Afrique."

Antoine wore only a t-shirt and shorts, as a wood stove provided more than enough heat. Helene couldn't help noticing the prominent tattoos displayed on his arms. One was a triangle with a scull in the middle. The top of the triangle held the word Legio and on the two sides were Patria and Nostra. She had been mostly silent since they had arrived but now she spoke up. "Antoine, I was going to ask you about your tattoos. Were you really in the French Legion? And I like the way you pronounce my name."

Antoine bustled behind the counter, making coffee. "I was born in New York in 1990 of an American father and French mother. In 2010, I went to France and only returned in 2035 when I was forty-five and too old for any more soldier games," he said, avoiding her question. He began to toast a croissant on his wood stove. "I've got a smaller stove that works off propane in the back, but I like this one, Old Betty. She makes the best coffee. Have you read the French-Algerian author, Albert Camus? You know he wrote something back in the 1950s that is particularly valid today."

"Who is he, and what did he say?" Helene asked.

"Camus was a famous French writer," he said. "He

wrote, 'In the depth of winter, I finally learned that within me there lay an invincible summer.'"

"That's beautiful," she said quietly.

When Helene teared up, Josh broke in. "Antoine," he said. "Make some omelets for these two, and then we can go out back and you can show me that beauty you brought home from La Legion."

"Mais oui," Antoine replied. "She will be well worth waiting for."

After breakfast, Antoine and Josh went out back. There "she" was, as promised, on a tripod set up on the back of Antoine's pickup truck. "That's an Eryx 50 short-range anti-tank missile launcher from around 2020," Josh said. "Portable, light, usable in urban areas, day or night, whatever the weather. It can also bring down low-flying helicopters. It works off battery cables not computer digital equipment. The same technology used in early twentieth century torpedoes."

"Bien sûr," Antoine replied. "I brought her back from La Legion in 2035. I had to pay to smuggle her out of North Africa and into the U.S. She's a museum piece, first used by La Legion in the early 2000s. This model remained in service a few more years until around 2040. I used her when I served with La Legion. She's the only thing I have left, along with my 9 mm MAC 50 pistol and some ammo. I clean and fire her once a month."

Josh asked, "Can you fire her for me?"

Antoine replied, "Désolé, but I've already fired her this month."

The two returned to the front of the café. Josh rounded up Helene and Tom and drove them to the campus to pick up their Harley. On the way back, Josh asked Tom, "How well do you know this area?"

When Tom explained the years he spent in school, his knowledge of the mountains behind Blacksburg, Christiansburg, and Radford, as well as the roads they had traveled from Roanoke, Josh said, "I want you to help me with our defensive plans."

For the next two weeks, Tom didn't see much of Helene as he was busy working with Josh on the defensive plans. He knew she was trying to figure out how to deal with what had happened on the road to Roanoke and then in Roanoke itself. He figured she would work it out; she was resilient and smart. He wanted to be supportive, but he knew he could never feel what she felt. He had never been in her situation. Nothing that bad had ever happened to him. Yes, they had both lost their parents and he would have to come to terms with that once he had the time.

When Helene cut her long raven hair short, Tom noticed. She now looked almost boyish. It was obvious that she wanted to be less vulnerable and thought the new haircut might help. He did find out that Helene was learning how to shoot a light machine gun, and Antoine was teaching her. *This might help her to release the pent-up aggression and anger at those who raped and imprisoned her,* Tom thought. For the first time in their lives, conversation was difficult, as she kept her thoughts to herself and didn't say much.

Helene was not silent with Antoine. She could confide in the older Frenchman, who was halfway between an older friend and a father, but also a complete stranger. She read somewhere that it was easier to talk to strangers about pain and personal things, and she was learning just how true that was. Antoine was someone who didn't know her and would not judge her.

One day she offered, "You know, Antoine, I'm not sure if there is any summer left in me. Things have happened that I would never have dreamed. I'm not just talking about Surge Saturday. There've been other things. You know that guy, Camus? What else did he write about?"

"Camus focused most of his books around existential questions like the absurdity of life and inevitability of death. He believed we are unable to know the meaning of life, but it is our duty to live a life of freedom and responsibility," Antoine said. "Camus defended the necessity for revolt against any kind of oppression or injustice. In one of his books, he wrote, 'I revolt, therefore we exist,' implying all of us share humanity and the duty to make things better. Mais chéri, peut-être c'est trop de philosophie pour une journée, hein ?"

"I like when you speak French to me," Helene said. "I got the *too much philosophy part*. And I think maybe Camus was right. All we have is our principles. But where do they come from and how do we defend them? When did he die?"

Antoine sighed. "He died in 1960 in a car crash. Totally absurd, isn't it?"

Tom saw his work with Josh as his way of fighting back. He remembered feeling so helpless when Black Sun killed those people on the Lafayette hill, when he saw the violence toward minorities and those of differing religions or sexual preference and did nothing. He was haunted by the memory of the day his sister was raped and he did nothing. In his studies of history, he had come across a quotation from British statesman Edmond Burke. "The only thing necessary for the triumph of evil is that good men should do nothing." Without a moment's hesitation, he plunged into the maelstrom. He would help Josh prepare for the Black Sun attack. With some preparation, they might have a chance of surviving.

Chapter 16
The Ops Plan

Tom and Josh took several days to choose suitable locations for the defense of Blacksburg. Finally, they picked one of the hills overlooking Route 460 west of Blacksburg to set up an observation post. They strengthened the roadblock at the destroyed bridge between Christiansburg and Blacksburg. They also positioned scouts in the Christiansburg area close to Route 81.

Josh and Commander Wilson decided to divide their men and weapons. The stronger force would protect against any enemy advance from Route 81 to the east, and a smaller force would defend the rear against infantry that could approach from the west. The fifty VT cadets, armed with light machine guns, rifles, and two light mortars, would post up to the west of Blacksburg along with a Humvee and a Cougar tactical vehicle. Commander Wilson decided to have Antoine's anti-tank Eryx and Josh's stinger missile support the cadets from the hills above.

The thirty National Guard troops and sixty former soldiers and volunteers, supported by a Humvee and a Cougar tactical vehicle, would take their position just west of the destroyed bridge. Equipped with the medium weight machine guns, rifles, shotguns, and mortars, the plan was to defend Blacksburg from the main Black Sun assault. Josh decided that they should move the Abrams tank to a ridge overlooking the former Blacksburg Bridge. It would remain stationary, as the engine was not in good shape.

It was not long before the militia's scouts saw a convoy moving along Route 81. They also located Black Sun scouts in Humvees moving parallel on Route 11 to the west of Route 81and to the east on Route 460. Two Apache helicopter gunships provided them with overhead support.

The night before the expected first engagement, Commander Wilson gathered everyone on the VT drill field. One hundred and forty against what was rumored to be over a thousand Black Sun troops. With both the American flag and the Cross and Crescent banner streaming in the wind behind him, the commander prepared to use the battery-operated field microphone. Tom and Helene exchanged looks. Helene could see the worry on her brother's face. The skin across his cheeks seemed too tight, and he squinted his eyes more than usual. Then she looked at the commander. "He looks older," she said. The commander prepared to speak from his elevated position near the old military chapel. He paused and wiped his forehead with a handkerchief. Then he began, his voice soft, trembling with emotion but becoming louder like an ancient Greek oracle.

"I know we probably can't defeat the force massed against us." At that moment, Tom had a sense of *déjà* vu.

Returning to reality, Tom heard, "We are not enough to win. Our task is to hold the line and slow them down. Many years ago, before our fallen Republic had become a great nation, a small group of rag-tag defenders at an old church held off a much larger force and bought time for the American resistance to organize and later win. Will you stand with me? Will you help our free city buy time for our comrades farther south?"

Standing to the left of Commander Wilson, Tom, Helene, and Josh heard a voice behind them shouting, "Aux armes citoyens." Words from the battle hymn of the French Republic. Antoine stepped up and joined them as they all saluted the flags.

Chapter 17
Aux armes citoyens

At six in the morning, the sounds of a helicopter gunship, several transport helicopters, and a transport plane droned through the air. They were all moving west toward the mountains behind Blacksburg, probably to drop equipment and troops. Helene and Tom had ridden their Harley to a cul-de-sac at the base of the hill Josh had pointed out earlier in the week. They parked next to Josh's jeep. "He must already be at the hill top position," Tom said, as they began their ascent.

Arriving at the rocky, almost barren summit, they took a position next to Josh under a small group of pine trees. He was checking the enemy's advance through his field glasses. He handed them to Tom and began to sight the

Stinger. Next, he laid the Stinger carefully on the ground and checked the action on the light machine-gun he carried. From their position on the top of a hill facing west, Tom and Helene could scan the mountain road below.

Fifty VT cadets spread out below them between two hills in a line across Route 460, with some men at the base of the slopes. Using Josh's field glasses, Tom looked north and saw Antoine positioning himself in a Cyprus-covered parking lot on a nearby hilltop. He was sighting his Eryx anti-tank missile launcher, which was positioned on the open truck bed.

Josh's radio squawked. It was Antoine. "Mon commandant has been trying to get through to you. He said two Chinook helicopters are dropping enemy soldiers to our west, and the troops are approaching our position. A cargo plane dropped two Humvees by parachute. They'll begin to advance east along Route 460 with an Apache gunship providing air support."

"How's the commander?" Josh asked.

Antoine continued, "He says the main Black Sun army supported by an Apache gunship, two Viper battle tanks and some Humvees, is advancing up the Christiansburg valley toward the bridge."

"Copy," Josh growled. "I'll radio the cadets below." He proceeded to call the cadet colonel while Tom checked his shotgun ammo and Helene shouldered her light machine gun in preparation for the attack.

The first weak rays of the orphaned sun hit the earth. The sunlight reflected on the frozen ground. Ice-covered pines glistened like a band of angels blazing with God's might.

As Black Sun forces began to engage the cadets along Route 460, an Apache gunship flew over them, firing several missiles. The cadets retreated from the more open ground beside the road to the rocky tree-lined slopes, where it was more difficult for the gunship to reach them. The Black Sun Chinook helicopters, having dropped off two loads of men, were returning to the east to pick up more. As they passed over, they also fired down on the cadets.

The cadets' light mortars shells took out one enemy Humvee, but there were too many Black Sun troops, and more Humvees were approaching. The situation looked hopeless.

As the Apache airship turned west back toward the mountains to make another pass over the cadets, it dropped to better target their position and circled lower over Antoine's hill top. He fired the short-burn Eryx anti-tank rocket from the bed of his truck and landed a direct hit on the Apache. It disappeared in flaming pieces.

The pilot in one of the two Chinooks, seeing the positon from which the missile launched, told his gunner to turn his turret gun on Antoine. The two siblings and Josh saw Antoine's truck explode in a burst of flames. The Chinook then prepared to return to the east for more men. As it flew over them, Helene, Tom, and Josh crouched under the trees. At just at the right moment, Josh stood, aimed, and fired the Stinger. The missile hit the Chinook's underbelly. It spun out of control, split apart, and fell in pieces into the gully below. Josh dropped the missile launcher and grabbed his radio. "Antoine, Antoine, are you there?"

No response.

Helene dropped her gun and sat on the ground, her head in her hands. Then she raised her head with a look of both despair and determination and said to no one in particular, "I will remember Antoine's invincible summer. We are truly invincible." She stood up and picked up her gun.

Commander Wilson was also on the channel. "Sergeant," he said, "We have been sustaining significant losses from tank fire and from an Apache gunship. They are making it easy for the enemy to advance on our position. Our Abram's tank got one of the enemy tanks, but their Apache took out the Abrams. The men are using the mortars to provide cover for our forces to fall back. We'll regroup in downtown Blacksburg and make our last stand on the Virginia Tech campus."

Josh responded, "We got one Apache and one Chinook, but the other Chinook will be returning with more troops. Their Humvees are advancing. Our cadets are taking losses. We are outnumbered. We won't be able to hold for long. We lost Antoine."

"Copy that." Commander Wilson responded. "Too bad about Antoine. We may soon join him. Are the two from Roanoke with you? If they are, get them the hell out of there. I want you to make sure they get to Atlanta. You know whom they need to talk to. That's my last command, son. Get the hell out. Good luck and Godspeed. Over."

"Let's get back to the vehicles," Josh said. "You heard the commander. You two will take the news to Atlanta. I'm gonna see that you get there. I'll lead in my jeep and provide covering fire. The two of you follow on the Harley. If we hit opposition, I'll take them head-on. You veer off and try to get through the lines. Got it?"

Tom blurted out, "We won't leave you behind, Josh."

Josh cut him off. "You heard me, kid. Just get on the bike and make it to Atlanta."

As the three made their escape, a pyrocumulonimbus "fire" cloud formed in the skies over the battlefront. The mortars and tank fire had lit the brush, and the fires were burning hot. The hot air and smoke quickly rose in a column, creating a turbulent atmosphere. A thunderstorm developed and heat lightning hit the ground, making it seem like fire was falling on both sides of the battle. The sky turned bright red.

Chapter 18
Escape

Josh drove his jeep toward Radford with the Harley in its wake. Taking back roads, they skirted the main enemy force deployed at Christiansburg near Route 81. Things went well until they reached Radford. A town of red, white, brown, and yellow painted brick buildings, it was home to Radford University, which had closed since that fateful Saturday in September 2050.

Radford's original, covered bridge crossing the New River was the site of a key battle during the American Civil War. A new steel structure had replaced the wooden bridge in the late 1940s, and two parallel steel bridges replaced that single bridge in the early 2000s. With one of the two bridges destroyed, Black Sun set up a roadblock on the parallel bridge. Two jeeps blocked the route and were positioned in such a way that the soldiers could check cars leaving or entering the city and fire at a threat from either direction.

A block from the bridge, Josh pulled over and parked on an abandoned side street. He knew they needed to cross the bridge in order to reach a section of Route 81 not controlled by Black Sun. As he turned off the jeep's motor, he motioned to the siblings to approach.

"I stopped because I have something to tell you. In case I don't make it, your contact in the Atlanta Resistance is the owner of the Shakespeare Tavern Playhouse. Don't know his name but your oral bona fides are the words, *hope* and *freedom*, used in a normal sentence like '*I hope Bob will get his freedom soon.*' Now stay behind me. I'm going to crash through the jeeps blocking the far end of the bridge. You need to move through the opening I provide, like a quarter-back threading his way through a hole made by his offensive guards."

Tom looked at his new friend and brother in this strange world. "We won't leave you, Josh," he said.

"We all go through together or we die together," Helene added. "We won't let those bastards win."

"Think with your heads. Who will let Atlanta know

what is happening? I'm counting on you two. Just do what I say. Soldiers all have to die sometime."

Josh restarted the jeep, and the two got on their Harley. He gunned the jeep's engine and accelerated across the bridge, driving straight at the two Black Sun jeeps. Josh immediately took on rapid fire from the Black Sun soldiers. Keeping his left hand on the wheel, he returned fire, using his machine gun propped on the jeep's dash. He was hit several times. Tom and Helene, moving closely behind, could see his body bounce backward against the seat from the force of the bullets. The former sergeant major managed to keep his vehicle on course and crashed through the middle of the jeeps, but his vehicle veered to the right. It went off the bridge, taking one of the jeeps with it. The other jeep spun into a tree. Tom found his window of daylight and pushed the Harley through. Helene fired her pistol left and right at the enemy soldiers. They made it, but without Josh. Helene wondered if he died before his jeep hit the water. They had no time to look back.

Just short of the entrance to Route 81, Helene told Tom to stop. "Pull over into the woods," she said. "No one has been following us. I've looked back for the last five miles. If they had tried to get ahead on Route 81, we would have already seen them from up here on the interchange below."

Helene got off the bike, took her backpack from the carrying case, opened the bag, and pulled out an old paperback book. Her hand trembled with rage as she held the book. There were tears in the corners of her eyes, but her voice was hard. Turning to her brother, she spat out her words. "Antoine gave me this. It was one of his prize possessions. He said it was by that guy, Camus. He wrote it during a time of affliction about one hundred years ago. Antoine told me that France was overrun by troops from Nazi Germany, a country that based its principles on the same type of garbage that Black Sun now chooses to believe. At the time, the French people made different choices. Some fled to London to join the British anti-Nazi war effort, while others chose to give up and accept their fate. A third group chose to resist. Camus likened the Nazi take-over to a plague, which is the title of this book. There's a passage I'd like to read in memory of Josh. I've underlined it. Camus says, 'What interests me is living and dying for whatever one loves.' Josh loved freedom, and he died for it."

Helene bowed her head. "Let's take a moment," she said. "The Vikings believed in Valhalla and the Christians believe in heaven. I don't know what I believe, but I would like to wish Josh a safe journey. Say hi to Antoine for me, Josh, if you should meet him in your travels."

The young woman got back on the bike. In a voice filled with a mixture of pain and determination, she said, "Let's go. We have someone to meet in Atlanta."

They reached Route 81 and drove south. Tom soon decided they needed to get off the highway to avoid Black Sun convoys. Wytheville, at the Route 21 exit, was their first chance. It would lead them to the old Blue Ridge Parkway, too winding, indirect, and now potentially too structurally dangerous for Black Sun convoys, but perfect for them.

A halfway point between Charleston, West Virginia and Charlotte, North Carolina, Wytheville became a commercial hub in the mid-1800s. After the Reconstruction Era, the majority white community reasserted its supremacy and, in 1926, the last pre-Black Sun lynching in the state took place there. A group of white men broke Raymond Bird, a black man, out of jail where he was awaiting trial. Then they shot him, dragged him for miles behind a truck, and hung his dead body from a tree, all because he was accused of having voluntary sex with a white woman. If they had known the town's history, the siblings would have found it no surprise that the citizenry now supported Black Sun. To the historical observer, the town had not changed, except Black Sun flags had recently replaced Confederate flags flown on the local porches.

The aging red-brick buildings, wooden houses, white porches with colored petunias in flower boxes, and the old general store were throwbacks to earlier times. As Helene and Tom needed supplies, they entered the store. They were surprised that the store was well- stocked with fresh vegetables, which apparently came from the local farmers. There also was an abundance of canned goods on the shelves.

In answer to the owner's greeting, Tom said, "This can go down one of two ways. Either we can shoot you and take what we want, or we can take what we want and, when we're done, give you this shotgun in exchange. I'm sure you'll want to have a weapon with what is going on these days."

The owner, looking at the shotgun barrel pointed at him, replied, "Take what you want. I'll take the gun."

Tom tossed the empty gun to the owner and began to put items in a basket while Helene pointed her light machine-gun at the man. They loaded up on canned goods, including beans and corn, as well as some bread and smoked ham. Tom also took a skillet, a metal knife, and a canteen.

Since the Harley's gas tank was nearly empty, they told the owner they needed petrol. With the machine-gun still trained on him, he replied nervously in his southwestern Virginia drawl, "You'd might be able to convince Abe Parker at the local gas station to give you some. But you'd better have something to trade. Abe might just take your head off. He got a shotgun too, yah know. Station's closed, but I know he got some gas stored out back for his pickup. She runs on gas and solar, but now it's just gas. These days the cloud cover doesn't let enough sunlight in. On rainy days, the batteries can't store much energy. It's a wonder the farmers can still grow crops. Go down Main Street, few blocks on the left."

As the two backed out of the store, Tom said, "I'll leave these shells with Abe Parker. You can pick them up there. I don't want to get shot in the back." They remounted the Harley and proceeded down the street.

Abe Parker, a gray-bearded, husky man with an old ball cap on his balding head, was sitting in front of his run-down establishment. He had a double-barreled shotgun on his lap and a thin hound dog at his feet. Tom asked him about gas. Abe replied, "Might have some. Whatchu got to trade for it? Money's worthless to me."

Helene knew the man would not take just her pistol in exchange, so she showed him the light machine gun and several ammo clips instead and kept the pistol. "We'll give you this for a full tank of gas for the Harley," she said.

Abe seemed too inquisitive. "Where you get that?"

"Found it near an abandoned gas station just off Route 81 near Christiansburg. Seems like a big battle was going on over there. We're on our way to Asheville to join the ranks of Black Sun in that city," Tom lied. The siblings filled the tank and loaded an extra gas can on the back. Tom placed the shotgun shells on the owner's desk. "These are for the grocery store owner. He'll be by in a bit." The two left in a hurry before Abe could ask any more questions. They accessed the Blue Ridge Parkway at Cherry Lane and began the trek south toward Asheville and Atlanta.

Chapter 19
Heading South

The two rode slowly as the many turns and bad condition of the highway made it too dangerous to let the Harley run full out. At mile marker 217, they found Cumberland Knob Visitor Center. Now abandoned, this Center had been a hub for hikers and birders who walked the trails through the former lush fields that had been full of wildlife, marsh birds, ducks, geese, bluebirds, robins, and thrush. It had been warmer then. Now, only the conifers retained their needle-like leaves. Although it was only early October, there were traces of snow on the ground and the other trees were leafless.

The two smashed a glass pane on the main door

and entered the Center, but found no water, just non-functioning bathrooms. Despite the smell of urine and human waste, which made the two want to vomit, it was a good place to get out of the cold and escape the coming night. Since they had left Blacksburg in a hurry, they had no sleeping bags and used the building's furniture to start a fire. Tom raided the garbage cans for paper, added what was left of toilet paper he found in the stalls, and surrounded the mound he made with twigs he found outside. As the wood outside was damp, they threw pieces of broken furniture on the fire. Later, they were able to add some of the logs. Helene cooked some baked beans. They drank water from their canteen and went to sleep. Early the next morning, they went south again.

On the afternoon of the next day, still hoping to find some water, they stopped at the Linville Falls Visitor Center. After searching in vain for water inside the building, they found a clear mountain stream that ran down from the hills above them. Before they'd filled their canteen, they checked for any potential hazardous sources and then positioned themselves downstream below some rocks. The stream flowed into a nearby pond, where mallards with bold emerald green and blue feathers dunked their heads for fish. A flock of white snow geese with black-tipped wings passed overhead, honking and heading south in a V formation.

Returning to the wooden gray-painted building, they noticed that there were various maps placed on a bulletin board next to the doorway. Like their previous stop, this had been an area for hiking. The maps detailed a large lake and waterfalls that fell in three tiers along the Linville Gorge, as well as the trails to Chimney Rock and Linville Caverns. Apparently, Black Sun had not come this way. Nothing had been touched.

Intrigued by the promised views, they were tempted to explore and take a break from the last days' emotional toll, but decided to focus on getting to Asheville instead.

"Hey," Helene said. "There is a sign at the entrance to the lot that reads: Asheville, sixty-five miles. Do you think we should spend the night?"

"I'm not sure," Tom said. "I think we'd better stay here and cover the remaining miles tomorrow. It's getting dark, and I don't know what we might face on the road ahead."

Nearby, they discovered an old camping area with tents formerly rented by vacationers. As the two approached the empty tents, they entered a large meadow surrounded by conifers on all sides. Suddenly, four white men with pump-action shotguns surrounded them. All four wore camouflaged hunting caps, pants, and jackets. The oldest-looking of the four approached them. His tangled mass of greasy gray and black hair sat lankly on his head. His untrimmed beard was stained with tobacco, and he was sucking on a twig. "Is that your Harley parked out in front?"

Another man, who appeared to be in his late forties and who resembled the first, but just a bit younger, spoke up. "Sam, look at that pretty thang. Haven't seen such a pretty thang in a while. Maybe we should take the Harley and the girl, and kill this boy." Speaking to the two teenagers behind him, who were pointing their shotguns at the siblings, he continued, "Boys, keep your guns trained on him while I check her for weapons. I think your Uncle Sam won't mind if I frisk the girl first. She must have something interesting concealed under that jacket and pants."

"Be my guest, Bill," Sam replied as he took off his hat like a comical musketeer and flourished it, pretending to bow to his brother.

Tom stepped in front of Helene and glared at the man. A cold sweat ran down his back. *Shit, shit, shit… we gave away our guns for food and gas.* Knowing Helene still had her pistol, he moved forward, but as he did, Sam approached him from behind and hit the back of Tom's legs with the shotgun. Tom went down hard. Helene slowly reached for the pistol she had hidden in the back of her jeans. This time, she was not going to submit without a fight.

Just then, Bill tumbled to the ground, an arrow buried in his back. Before Sam could turn, he was struck in the neck by a second arrow. He fell to his knees, blood gushing from the hole made by the arrow's metal tip. The tip protruded out the front of his neck just below his Adam's apple. In their haste to avoid further arrows, which seemed to come from nowhere, Bill's two youngsters ran. They didn't look back until they made the tree line. Once there, they turned, looked, and kept running.

It didn't take Sam long to die. Bill was still squirming on the ground when a tall young man with a bow slung over his shoulder walked out of the woods behind the clearing. He was dressed in leather moccasins, jeans, and a wool poncho. A deerskin headband with one eagle feather was tied around his long dark braided hair. The sheen from his hair and the glow of the sunrays dancing on the sharp metal knife-blade he carried gave him an unworldly appearance. He checked the tree line for the boys, but they had disappeared. Then he slit Bill's throat as the siblings watched in amazement.

With her hand still clutching her pistol, Helene kept her eyes on the stranger while she reached down and helped her brother get to his feet. She opened her mouth as if to say something to the stranger, but he spoke first. "These men are rabid dogs and they deserved to die before they can spread their sickness any further."

Her frown of disapproval disappeared. "Yes, I guess they did deserve to die, but I would have just shot them. Thanks for your help, though. I wouldn't have let them take me, you know. I would have died first."

"I could see that," the young man responded. "My name is William Blackstone. You can call me Waya. It means wolf in Cherokee. I am part of Cherokee Nation of South Appalachia. I come from Conaluflee Village, Qualla Boundary Reservation in Great Smoky National Park. Since the rise of many waters and the birth of the gray thunder mountains which closed the heavens, I have been on a quest to find a way to heal the sky."

Waya had a habit of talking in stereotypic Indian-speak which is the way he assumed all whites thought Indians talked. It was a defense mechanism, which gave him an advantage in social engagements.

Tom offered his hand. "Tom Rogers," he said, "and this is my sister Helene. We're trying to get to Asheville and then the coast, so we can find a boat to take us to Atlanta. We need to stop some very evil people; a lot worse than these two you killed. They want to enslave the world under their rule."

"I've heard of these people," Waya responded. "They are the ones who bring a darkness that spreads over the land. My ancestors predicted what has come to pass. We serve the Creator Spirit who made all people one with plants, animals, and beasts. We pray to the omnipotent, omnipresent, and omniscient Creator who provides for His children. But these dark ones are descendants of those who have sown the whirlwind. They and their ancestors have displeased the Creator.

"As predicted since early days, the time for the world's end has arrived with water and showers of fire. Is it not so? But I will find a way, with my ancestors, to open the windows of heaven, and return the earth to the harmony of all beings."

"We want to stop them too," Helene replied. "We can work with each other. Will you help us get to Asheville?"

"It seems we share a common journey, Helene Rogers. I will take you there," Waya responded. "My horse is not far. I will get him and ride in front of your motorcycle."

Just after Waya killed the two men, the sun disappeared and was replaced by dark clouds. "It seems a storm is brewing, so we better leave now," Waya continued. "We will follow this road to Asheville."

While Waya went to retrieve his horse, Tom and Helene gathered the dead men's two pump-action shotguns, a Remington and a Mossberg. Tom felt a new warmth inside. They could defend themselves again. Unfortunately, when they checked for ammunition, they found only ten and eight shotgun shells respectively on the men's bodies.

Waya, riding his gray stallion, Thunder, led the way to Asheville.

Chapter 20
Asheville to the Sea

The city of Asheville was originally built on Cherokee land. The Europeans who established the city brought diseases, and in the ensuing years, they seriously depleted the native population. Later, Asheville became a flourishing commercial area in the 1950s and was reborn in the early 2000s as a vacation resort/retirement community. This was due to the many outdoor sports activities and the huge Biltmore Estate. This Chateauesque-style mansion, built by George Washington Vanderbilt II in 1895, continued to be owned and operated by his descendants until Surge Saturday. Over the last few weeks, Ashville had become a

Black Sun stronghold, and the Biltmore had been chosen as the local Black Sun headquarters.

Due to the color of Waya's skin and the recent events in Blacksburg, the three travelers decided that it would not be wise to stay in Asheville. They quickly bypassed the city and took the road to Hendersonville, twenty-two miles farther southeast. At first, the siblings found it difficult to follow the Cherokee on horseback. Tom finally got the hang of keeping the Harley in rhythm with Thunder's gait. Once they arrived in Hendersonville, the trio found an abandoned barn with peeling red paint and wood that was disintegrating with age. They pulled the Harley inside and Waya stabled his horse. He took a bag of oats from his leather bag and fed Thunder. The three of them started a small fire, cooked some beans on their skillet, and went to sleep.

The next morning, they walked over to the Hendersonville Courthouse, a brick three-story, gold-domed building built in the classical style with six white pillars gracing the front. The three were on high alert. Helene had her revolver slipped into the back of her pants with the safety left on. Waya hid his knife under his poncho. They had hidden the shotguns and Waya's bow and arrows under a blanket. If Black Sun was around, they needed to be careful. They worried that with no electricity and computers down, they would not be able to access a map of the region to determine the best way to the coast. Fortunately, there were no Black Sun soldiers, and they found a recently sketched map of the new Southeast Coast of the U.S. posted on a bulletin board. It looked like others also wanted to find the best way to access the new coastline.

When the low lands of North Carolina disappeared, along with much of South Carolina and Eastern Georgia, a new triangular peninsula was formed. Greensborough, North Carolina now sat on the northeast side of the peninsula, Charlotte was located on the tip of the obtuse triangle, and the new port of Greenville, South Carolina was now located on the southwestern coast where the peninsular met the mainland.

The trio's plan was to leave the mountains after Hendersonville and move in a diagonal line across North Carolina and parts of South Carolina to reach the new port of Greenville, South Carolina. From Hendersonville, their current location, the Port of Charlotte was too far and possibly too dangerous a route for them. Josh had told them back in Blacksburg that he believed it was under Black Sun control. They hoped to secure a boat in

Greenville and sail the coast from Greenville past Athens, Georgia to Atlanta-Macon. This was the new principle Georgia port. By not traveling farther down the Blue Ridge, they would avoid days of overland travel and the difficult task of finding needed gas for their motorcycle.

The trip from Hendersonville to Greenville was uneventful. Waya told Tom and Helene during their journey that the area surrounding Greenville had originally been part of the hunting grounds of the Cherokee Nation and off limits to colonists. During the Revolutionary War, the area played a role in the war between the British and the colonists. The Cherokee who sided with the British did not come out well in this engagement, and the colonists built a town on their land, which eventually became Greenville.

Helene, still trying to deal with the deaths of Josh and Antoine, brooded in silence. She was also not sure about this Indian, this Cherokee. *This is a temporary alliance of necessity, but can he be trusted? He had saved their lives. He is also very handsome.*

As they arrived in town, they could see that Greenville had once been a center for clothing manufacture. Broken down cotton mills sat derelict and empty outside the town. Downtown, there was a convention center that gave the impression that the town had once tried to recover. However, the building had seen better days and needed substantial repair. Although Black Sun did not appear to be yet in control of Greenville, their symbols dotted many walls as the trio proceeded through the city.

They immediately searched for the Town Hall. A man they met on the street told them they could go there to find information on procuring passage on a ship. The town hall, a nine-story metallic-looking high rise, had become a business center for trade moving up and down the coast. Though Greenville had fallen on hard times, the Town Hall was proof that Surge Saturday had brought a rejuvenation of sorts.

Located at the foot of the Blue Ridge Mountains, Greenville had been high enough to avoid being submerged by the water from Surge Saturday. It was now a port city and a new commercial hub.

"I read something about this town when I was in high school," Waya said. "Back in 1947, thirty white cab drivers lynched a black man accused of stabbing a white cabbie. Apparently there was a trial, but no one was declared guilty."

Remembering the Black Sun symbols placed on the buildings they passed, Helene said, "This town hasn't changed. Black Sun will prosper here."

When the trio entered the Town Hall, it seemed to be a hub of activity. The section of the first floor was reserved for ship captains who were hiring crew and selling passage on various ships docked in the new bay. From one of the boat captains the travelers learned that a riverboat sternwheeler named the Louisiana Queen was leaving for Macon-Atlanta later that afternoon. Old steamboats, which until recently floated on lakes in historic parks or were used as river restaurants, had once again become a principle mode of transport. Boats that used gasoline were too expensive to run, even if gasoline was available. There were other boats in the harbor, but none were leaving that day or going south.

As the siblings had nothing to trade for their passage but their shotguns, Waya pulled out a gold piece and plunked it down on the counter. "This and the shotguns should pay for a cabin for the three of us," he said.

An elderly woman dressed in a frilled skirt and carrying a yellow parasol stood behind them in line. Although her hair was gray, she had an ageless quality and her violet eyes, matching the color of her dress, seemed to look right through them and the captain. When the three had finished negotiating their passage, she stepped forward and said, "I have just enough to book passage to Macon-Atlanta. Will you take me?" She pulled out a small wad of former U.S. currency and handed it to the captain.

"What will I do with that?" He pushed the valueless money back in her direction.

With tears in her eyes, she reached behind her neck and unclasped a silver necklace. Attached to it was a heavy cross of solid silver. "Will this do?"

"Sold," said the Captain. "Welcome aboard. We leave at five." In response, she bowed her head, walked out of the room, and disappeared.

Chapter 21
The Louisiana Queen

The Louisiana Queen was a paddle wheeler of the type once used widely on rivers in the nineteenth century. She burned wood and her iron boilers produced the steam that propelled her. Two smokestacks released gray plumes into the sky. They called her a stern paddleboat because her wheel was not on the side but at the rear of the boat. The first of her three decks consisted of a grand salon with tables, chairs, sofas, gambling room, and dining hall. Below that were the engine room, crew berthing quarters, and all equipment that made the boat function. The second deck was composed of rooms of various sizes, many with verandas that overlooked the water. There was also the Captain's cabin and the officers' stateroom. The wheelhouse was situated at the top of the ship.

There was no pilot in the wheelhouse as the captain piloted the ship. He had a crew of ten men to work the boilers, man the decks, and keep the ship afloat. The men lacked the old-fashioned fancy uniforms with gold braid and just wore jeans, sweatshirts, and jackets. Dinner was what the passengers brought to eat. The silk curtains in the parlors were torn and dirty; most of the velvet chairs were gone. The gambling tables had disappeared and the kitchen, which once served extravagant food, was empty except for what the crew needed for the duration of the two-day trip. That was how long it would take the boat to sail along the coast, which now included the parts of South Carolina and Georgia not under water.

Ten people had paid passage, and all of them claimed cabins on the second deck. Many of them appeared to be anxious to leave Greenville. The trio wonder if they were afraid that Black Sun would take over the city. There was one bathroom down the hall, but as they passed other passengers on their way to it, Helene noticed that no one spoke and people mostly looked at the ground, afraid to engage in conversation.

Tom, Helene, and Waya's cabin had one bed and a sink with no running water. It also had a small wood stove with a pipe that ran through the ceiling and up to the roof. The stove heated the room and could be used for cooking as well.

Waya offered to sleep in the hallway or down below in one of the remaining chairs in a first deck parlor, but Tom and Helene agreed that, for safety reasons, they should remain together. The two men ceded the bed to Helene and went in search of two mattresses. They found them in an empty bedroom down the hall and dragged them into their room. They could negotiate to pay more if the captain showed up and demanded extra payment. All agreed that one would stand guard while the other two slept.

Sounding its foghorn, the ship pulled out of the harbor late in the evening. As it got dark, the siblings lit candles in their room and, from their balcony, watched a shadow moon hanging over the calm inland sea. For the moment, all seemed peaceful.

The next morning, they noticed the older lady from the Greenville Town Hall sitting on the balcony next to theirs. She had woken early and was saying her morning prayers and communing with the gulls perched on the balconies next to hers. As Tom looked over, he saw one of the gulls, gray and white with dark speckles on its body, pecking at a kernel of corn she had placed on her railing. His leg seemed broken as he hopped over to the kernel using only one leg. "You're one of God's wondrous creatures," she said to the bird, "and He loves you very much." The bird took the kernel and then moved along the railing, now using two strong legs.

Tom looked again, and then assumed he was mistaken about the bird having been hurt, especially when he saw it take flight. "Good morning," he said to the lady. "I'm Tom Rogers and this is my sister Helene."

"Good morning to you," she said as Helene and Tom came out to look at the sea. "What a wonderful day. God's day. I'm Mary Burk, and I'm going to Atlanta by way of the port of Macon. The Lord has called me to preach there."

"Are you a pastor?" Tom asked. "Excuse me, but you don't look like the ones I've seen."

"You can call me that," she replied. "I believe that we all have a pastor within us. We all are here to minister to our brothers' needs. The Master said, 'I am the light of the world' and that we could do what he did." As she gestured at the gray sky still covered in ash dust, she said,

"All the greed, the pollution of God's world, the needless sentencing of our brothers to suffer, the anger and hatred, have caused this. But it is still God's day, and if we continue to pray and be obedient to His will, someday we will see the bright sun shine again."

"She's right," Waya said as he walked out to join the siblings. "The Great Spirit made us brothers and sisters. We were meant to live in harmony with plants and animals, not destroy them with pollution. But I'm still not sure how we restore the world to its original path. That is my quest. Perhaps Mrs. Burk also is on a quest?"

"Yes," she responded. "Macon-Atlanta is my Nineveh, but I am no Jonah."

Waya waved his hand at Mrs. Burk and said, "My name is Waya of the Cherokee, and it is my pleasure to make your acquaintance, Mrs. Burk. I believe in the one we call the Great Spirit."

Mrs. Burk replied, "A pleasure to meet you, Waya. I also believe in the one God who's called by many names. According to the Bible, He created all that is good. That is what the great teacher taught us. It's why he came to this world, to show us how to live in purity and peace."

Tom broke in. He was hesitant, but somehow he trusted this woman. "Hey, Mrs. Burk, you ever heard of the Cross and Crescent? I heard they believe that the world can be restored by those who think correctly. They believe all this mess has been created by evil, selfish thoughts, and we can un-think the disastrous results by letting pure thoughts control us."

Mrs. Burk replied. "It's not that simple. We can't un-think something. We need to challenge evil with the power of good. We need to see the face of God where evil seems to be. It's up to every one of us now."

Waya waited for Mrs. Burk to finish. "The evil ones must be punished," he said. "Those who have brought this down upon us must be destroyed. Then we will open the windows of heaven."

"Dear one," Mrs. Burk gently chided, "Heaven is within each of us. Giving in to their hate and fear will not rid us of evil. Only love will."

Helene interrupted the three-way conversation. "I'm hungry. What have we got to eat?"

"Bread and ham," Tom replied. "Mrs. Burk, you are welcome to share our food."

"I'll be right over with two eggs I traded for before we left Greenville. Something told me to get them even though I have nothing to cook them with."

Tom cut the ham and put bits of it in the skillet to

grease it for the eggs. He put the skillet on the wood stove and dropped in the first egg. They all listened to the hissing sound of the egg hitting the boiling ham fat. Tom dropped the second and let the yoke and white begin to form and harden before mixing them with the ham. He scooped out some of the mixture and put it on a slice of bread he had cut. Mrs. Burk, as the guest, got the first slice, then Helene, and then he served himself. Waya, who had politely declined their offer of food, watched the process while taking handfuls of something that looked like homemade granola and washing it down with water from a leather pouch.

"So, Mrs. Burk," Helene said. "Tell us something about yourself."

"Not much to tell, dear. I was born in the White Mountains of New Hampshire in 1985 and when I was seventeen, I went to Boston and attended the New England Conservatory of Music. That's when I first came into contact with the book."

"What book?" Helene asked.

"Why, *Science and Health*, of course. A New Hampshire woman, Mary Baker Eddy, who later founded a religion and an International Church in Boston, wrote it in the late 1880s. I visited the church once while I was studying there a long time ago. But I moved away to Washington, D.C. and taught music in the inner-city schools. I then went into social work. I never stopped reading the book. It has been my constant companion all these years, through hard and good times. I like it because it begins 'To those leaning on the sustaining infinite, today is big with blessings.' The Lord has never ceased to bless me when I've trusted him."

"Can you still trust Him with all that has gone on?" Tom asked.

"Tom's right," Waya added. "The evil ones must be stopped. Then the Great Spirit will forgive us for what we have done to His earth."

"I think He already has," Mrs. Burk said. "His grace is there for all of us if we accept it."

"I don't think Black Sun wants His grace," Helene offered.

The breakfast finished, Mrs. Burk thanked them profusely and returned to her room. They didn't see her again until later in the afternoon, when disaster threatened.

Chapter 22
The Waterspout and Mesocyclone

Waya was saying something about Mrs. Burk being a very nice lady who lived in a world of dreams when the sky darkened. Storm clouds appeared, and a columnar reddish vortex arose from the sea like a whirling tornado. If it were ancient times, mariners might have thought it was a great red dragon or sea serpent. Most waterspouts don't suck up water but this one did, and it was heading directly at the paddle wheeler. The sound was deafening, and the ship began to shake and wobble.

"What the hell is that?" Tom yelled as his mind flashed back to the short story about the *Garden of Time*. For a moment, he was back at the castle with the Count and

Countess but without a crystal flower to turn back time and make this advancing menace recede. The ship's alarm bell sounded.

"What should we do?" Helene shouted. Her eyes widened, her eyebrows moved upward in astonishment and disbelief, and adrenaline began to pour through her veins.

"We can do nothing," Waya replied. "We are in the hands of the Great Spirit. It is His will."

Just then, a voice both soft and strong spoke from the adjacent balcony. Mrs. Burk stood facing the whirling column. "You are not part of God's universe. I can see through you. I see only Love's face."

"What's she trying to do?" Waya said.

The waterspout began to move away. Tom's jaw dropped in amazement. Then, just as suddenly as it had appeared, it was gone. In spite of the ash cloud, a brilliant rainbow appeared over the horizon and broke through the gray sky. For a moment, the dark clouds disappeared and pink and gold hues replaced them. The three remained in stunned silence. Tom finally spoke. Reaching in his bag for his mom's New Testament, he gasped, "Who the hell is this woman?" He began to leaf through it, looking for a story he remembered. It was about Jesus, asleep on a boat and woken by his fearful disciples during a tremendous storm. Tom remembered how Jesus arose and stilled the storm. *Which Gospel was it in?* Tom couldn't remember.

The three of them rushed out of their cabin and knocked on Mrs. Burk's door. "It's open," she said. "Come in please."

"Did you see that waterspout?" Tom asked, hoping to get her to talk about the situation. "It almost engulfed the ship."

"Don't worry, dear. It's gone now. Go back to your cabin. Everything is fine."

As the three returned to the cabin, they passed the boat's First Officer who was coming down the hallway. He was white as a bedsheet and passed them without a comment. Fear had made him dumb. The Captain had sent him to check on the passengers, but he looked like someone needed to check on him. Once he passed them, the three entered their cabin and retired for the evening. After a restless night, they prepared to disembark in Macon early the next morning.

As the paddle wheeler pulled into port, it passed the remains of a wind turbine some twenty-seven miles off shore. There had been a row of them, but the tsunami had left only one partly standing. It stood silent like some three-legged metallic spider or futuristic scarecrow, perhaps an omen of things to come.

Chapter 23
The Port of Macon

The city of Macon thrived over the years because of its location on the Ocmulgee River. Plantation owners had used slave labor to farm cotton and depended on ships to take their product to market. In 1843, steamboats and the railroad increased their ability to reach a wider market. In the twentieth century, Macon grew into a prospering central Georgia city and served as a transportation hub for the entire state. The town became a thriving river-city whose skyline remained low, lacking Atlanta's overbearing tall buildings. When the tidal wave swept across the Georgia coastal plain, Macon, formerly over 300 feet above sea level, now sat at the shore of an inland sea extending from the former coastline of Georgia to the former Central Plain.

In the new world, the steam engine fulfilled the same function as the steamboats on the rivers and sea. Within weeks of Surge Saturday, workers had repaired the old eighty-mile railway line to Atlanta and service began between the two cities. There was evidence of Black Sun activity in Macon and recruiting stations spread throughout the city. However, the main seat of Black Sun power in the southeast was Atlanta. The travelers were headed for the belly of the beast.

People used to say that Macon was a livable city whose pink summer night skies made life pleasant and enjoyable. Now, the sky was covered by a mass of gray. It rained almost every other day. They were not sorry to leave Macon for Atlanta and departed several hours after they arrived.

Tom and Helene sold their motorcycle to another steamboat passenger who disembarked with them. They used one of the gold pieces they received to pay for their passage on the steam engine. Waya took a gold piece from his leather pouch and used it to buy passage for himself and Thunder. Then he used his last gold piece to buy Mrs. Burk a train ticket. She was so grateful it made the Cherokee uncomfortable. She said she would pray for him and would repay him once she got to Atlanta and found a way to support herself. Apparently, she was not only a preacher, but also a good seamstress. Tom idly recalled that the Apostle Paul had been a tentmaker.

The almost two-hour trip to Atlanta was uneventful, for which everyone was grateful.

Chapter 24
Atlanta

Formerly one of the major cities east of the Mississippi, Atlanta stood at an elevation of 750 to 1100 feet. The city had been 200 miles inland from the eastern seaboard of the United States and not been touched by the great tidal wave that flowed across much of eastern Georgia.

With the electric grid and satellites non-functioning, Atlanta had no internet, no working computers, no functioning cell phone towers, and no working phone lines. The city no longer had a functioning light rail. Without gas for private vehicles, there were almost no cars moving along the streets. Electric and solar-run buses had stopped running, and most people walked. The city population had been cut in half during weeks since Surge Saturday; first by lack of clean water that produced cholera, and then the Bolivian plague generated by garbage and rat-bite fever. Overrun and without electricity, the hospitals were doomed to fail.

A column of Black Sun soldiers had marched into Atlanta two weeks earlier. Unwilling to wait for a division from the north to move south, Black Sun's Western Command at Albuquerque had sent a brigade of 3,500 men from Austin, Texas. It took them a week in their gas-run troop carriers to get to Atlanta. A convoy of water trucks and gasoline tankers carrying petrol from the Special Petroleum Reserve (SPR) in Austin accompanied them. The Black Sun provisional government of Texas now controlled the SPR. The reserve, formerly in Houston until two years earlier, still had over eight hundred million barrels stockpiled outside Austin near Walnut Creek. Black Sun, who controlled and pumped the product, restricted use of gasoline to their military and the local police under their control.

When the Black Sun troops took over Atlanta, they set up a command post at Georgia State University. The first thing the Army did was to clear the garbage, burn the dead, and distribute clean water. Things got better, but people still needed jobs and food. Crowds milling around everywhere were like ants on an anthill. So was the ever-vigilant Black Sun surveillance.

Black Sun protected their military vehicles, equipment, and petroleum trucks by storing them inside the Georgia State University Arena. This base on the campus was less than five blocks from the State Capitol, which had become the administrative center for the new Black Sun Regional Governor. As the Governor had not yet been appointed, the Governor's mansion remained empty.

Tom gave Waya one of his two hoodies to help cover his hair and face. It replaced the Indian's hand-woven wool sweater. This enabled the three of them to move around in relative obscurity. Since Waya had no place or resources to keep his horse, Thunder, he had to sell his four-legged companion. He made a deal with a fellow passenger, a wealthy businessman, who left the train one stop before Atlanta. Waya received three small diamonds in return. A horse, especially a good one, was worth at least that much. Waya told the others, "At least I found him a good home where he will be cared for, fed, and not mistreated." Nevertheless, it was apparent from his demeanor he would miss his friend.

Once they arrived at the downtown Atlanta station, the three quickly lost track of Mrs. Burk. They were separated in the crowd. She had given them no forwarding address. All they knew was that she was going to find work as a seamstress. After searching for lodging, they decided to stay at a local hotel and paid two weeks' rent in advance. The city of Atlanta ran the building and guests stayed if they had something of value to barter. Waya paid with the first of the diamonds he received from the sale of Thunder. The apartment-hotel was located at a former student dorm on the Georgia Technical Institute campus and had a wood-burning stove with piping that led to the roof. The travelers still had enough diamonds left to barter for food for the next few weeks.

Lodging secured, their priority was to locate *The Shakespeare Tavern Playhouse*. They agreed that afterwards they would try to find Mrs. Burk.

After the incident with the waterspout, Tom wanted to believe the things she had said. He told the others, "There is something different about that woman, perhaps even mystical."

Helene was more skeptical and still undecided. "I saw it, but I still don't understand it."

Waya just liked Mrs. Burk.

After trading their canteen for a paper street map of Atlanta, they located the tavern's address on Peachtree Avenue near Renaissance Park. That was easy. Finding Mrs. Burk, on the other hand, would be like looking for a small diamond in a quartz quarry.

They were glad they had paid for their travel with the two shotguns. If discovered in their room or if they were stopped on the street, they would cause them to be suspect and perhaps investigated.

The next morning, moving east across town, they passed the old Coca Cola Building, the former CNN Broadcast Building, and Tech Square. Helene was amazed at the number of people living on the streets. Bewildered by their new reality, this once bustling mass of humanity walked aimlessly. Several Black Sun military enlistment centers seemed to be the hubs of activity with signs in front that read, *Join now. Two uniforms, three meals a day, and a place to sleep.* Large groups of young people stood in line out front. After walking for an hour, the travelers arrived at *The Shakespeare Tavern Playhouse.*

Chapter 25
The Tavern

There was no performance at the moment, but the tavern was open. The sign in front of the Tudor-looking building stated there would be a play performed that evening. The dark wood framing on the windows and the white stucco walls made the building look like it had been built in Shakespeare's day. The majestic entrance consisted of two solid oak doors with small windows and iron-circle door handles.

Helene opened one door and the others followed her inside. The designer had built the stage to resemble a two-story castle, which faced the audience. Management had placed dining tables in a semi-circle around the stage on the ground floor. Some waiters were setting up tables for that night's one-course dinner. In the brand new world, restaurants could not afford to serve more than one entrée and dessert. Tables were also located to the right and left of the stage on balconies. At the tavern's entrance was a small bar.

Hiding under his hoodie, Waya held back while Helene and Tom approached the bartender. "Is the owner around?" Tom asked.

"Who wants to know?" the man replied.

"We've got mutual friends in Blacksburg," Helene replied.

The tall, forties-looking bartender, sporting a pencil moustache and goatee, looked them over carefully before saying, "I'm the owner. My name is Charles Roberts. What can I do for you?"

Helene gave her version of the coded sentence Josh had provided. "Your friend Bob says to tell you he hopes to get down to see you soon. As soon as his wife gives him some freedom to travel."

The owner looked around to make sure none of the waiters could overhear them. He appeared to have a good reason to keep the conversation private. "I would love to see him," he said, "but it's dangerous to travel now. Wouldn't want him to put himself in danger just to see me. Have a drink on the house."

"We'll just take two Cokes and a water," Tom replied, as Waya nodded in agreement. Roberts disappeared into a back room to get the drinks.

When Roberts came out, he said, "Had the Cokes from before the Surge. Drink up."

The rather warm drinks came with cardboard coasters decorated with ink sketches of Shakespeare. Tom handed the Coke to Helene while Waya indicated he preferred the water. Motioning to Tom's drink, the owner said, "I put a lemon slice with yours. It's on the coaster." The lemon was rotten and the slice had greenish-white mold covering the peel.

As Tom took the slice and moved it onto the counter top, he realized something was scribbled in pencil on the coaster. It read, "*Can't talk. Under Black Sun surveillance. Get out now and don't come back. Lost cause.*" Tom then asked the owner, "Can I keep the coaster as a memento of this place? I like the ink drawing of Shakespeare." He then passed the coaster to Helene, who showed it to Waya.

"Help yourself," Roberts replied. "Got some work to do on stage. Nice talking with y'all." He walked away, leaving them to their drinks.

Helene murmured to the others, "Let's finish our drinks and go look for Mrs. Burk. Renaissance Park's near here and we can sit and rest a bit before we decide where we should look. We can also see if we are being followed, as the park will be more open than the street."

Drinks finished, the three went outside and walked south on Peachtree. They turned east on Pine Street and found the expansive Renaissance Park just ahead at the intersection of Pine and Piedmont. Entering the park, they strolled for a short distance and came to a paved square surrounded by what was once a garden. The previous spring, tulips of various shades, Bradford pears, dogwoods, and white and pink-blossomed cherry trees had ruled a pastel fairy kingdom. Now the garden stood isolated and barren. The white, red, and pink azalea plants would never bloom. Frozen in time, they awaited the impossible arrival of a brighter day and warmer sun.

A large crowd had gathered in the square, shouting and waving their fists at someone. In the center of the hostile crowd stood an elderly woman. The woman asked for calm, so she could address them. "I would like to quote Mary Baker Eddy, a great religious leader of the nineteenth and twentieth century. Eddy wrote, 'Citizens of the world, accept the glorious liberty of the sons of God and be free. This is your divine right.' My friends, we can all be free if we resist bigotry, hatred and intolerance." Various bystanders began to throw empty bottles and cans at her. The jeering crowd tried to drown out her voice, shouting, "Blasphemer!" "African-lover!" "Communist!" "Lesbian!"

"That looks like Mrs. Burk," Waya said. It was indeed Mrs. Burk, and she was holding one arm in front of her head to shield herself from the flying cans and bottles. "We've got to get her out of there before she gets hurt." He began elbowing his way through the crowd.

As Waya moved forward, five equestrian police officers with Black Sun armbands rode in from the other side and dispersed the crowd in all directions. Tom, Helene, and Waya had to move back. They could not get to Mrs. Burk, who was now surrounded by police. A van drove up and other police officers quickly bundled her into it and departed, leaving the three wondering how to react.

Helene turned to a nearby woman who had been in the crowd. "What will they do with that blasphemer?"

"Most likely they'll take her to the Atlanta Municipal Courthouse. That's where Black Sun takes all dissidents and criminals."

"Where exactly is that located?" Helene asked.

"Over from the Capitol Building down on Garnett. Why?"

"I just want to see her get what she deserves. Will there be a public trial?"

"There are no public trials, only public executions. Just walk down Piedmont to the Capitol Building, pass Black Sun Plaza, and turn right on Memorial. You'll come up behind it. I hope they hang that bitch."

"Thanks," Helene said. "I hope so too."

Chapter 26
To Save Mrs. Burk

When the woman had gone, Helene, Tom, and Waya exited the park and turned south on Piedmont. The three were silent, their heads down, focused on the ground as they walked. "I thought I saw her heal a bird's leg," Tom said. "Did you see that, Helene, the first morning on the riverboat? I could have sworn the bird was hopping on one leg until after it went to get a kernel of corn from her balcony. After she spoke with it, it moved freely on two feet. I thought I was mistaken at the time, but then after the waterspout… and what she said about how we could change the world…"

Helene cut in. "I think she is special too, Tom. I'm just not sure if she is totally believable. What she said about that book she carries and the fact that God has blessings in store for us… to overcome evil with good."

Waya, who had been deep in thought, spoke up. "I still think the evil ones must be punished, but I have to admire that lady. She will give her life for what she believes."

Tom responded, "Just now, it sounded like she wasn't afraid of Black Sun. She challenged its intolerance. We've got to save her. But how?"

When they passed Auburn Street, they saw an old broken sign indicating the Ebenezer Baptist Church was several blocks to the east. "Can we detour a bit?" Tom asked. "We can't do anything for Mrs. Burk until we find out what they'll do with her. I'd like to see where Martin Luther King, Jr. preached. He fought for the rights of African-Americans. Maybe the parishioners will help us save Mrs. Burk. Maybe if we told them about Mrs. Burk and how she believes in equality and justice for all, maybe they would agree to help. That is, if they still believe what the Reverend preached about justice and equality."

The detour was in vain. The church had been destroyed. All that remained of the inside wooden structure was charred ruins. The roof was gone. The brick façade was broken in many places. The structure was just an empty shell. From the looks of the damage, this destruction appeared to have been a recent event. A Black Sun flag was planted across the street at the entrance to the former Martin Luther King Park. A newly painted sign read *Aryan Race Park*. The three quickly backtracked to Piedmont and continued south, passing the state Capitol and former Freedom Park, now Black Sun Park. At the center of the park, a large Black Sun flag fluttered in the breeze. After walking for another fifteen minutes, they arrived at the courthouse.

The Atlanta Municipal Courthouse was composed of two sections of a large rectangular building, which bookended on each side the entrance with its two-story blue glass cupola. Four stone columns, each two-stories high, supported the cupola. Marble stairs ascended to the entrance. The rectangular sections of the building, made of white stone, included two four-paned glass windows per floor. Decorative columns beginning on the third floor rose to outside the fifth. The building's entrance, located on Garnett Street, sat across from a multi-story unused public garage. The former Atlanta police station, now occupied by Black Sun police, sat to the west across Pryor Street. Waya noticed it immediately. "Those are the people who arrested Mrs. Burk. This does not look good."

As they walked past a square that sat near the courthouse's main entrance, a large sign announced, "Public executions tomorrow." Crossing the street to the public parking garage and climbing to the second floor, they used the binoculars Josh had given them to surveil the courthouse's main door.

After about an hour, three police officers exited the courthouse, escorting Mrs. Burk and two other prisoners. All three prisoners were handcuffed. The first man wore a yarmulke and a white scarf with the Star of David embroidered on the front. The second man was dressed in a rounded black cap and green robe. Helene said, "The first guy looks like a rabbi and the second appears to be an imam. I guess their intolerance doesn't discriminate. They want to eliminate all religions and replace them with their white Aryan apocalyptic garbage."

The travelers quickly returned to the street outside the garage and inserted themselves into a crowd of people walking by the courthouse. The three moved slowly behind the crowd, who yelled insults at the prisoners.

"I hope they hang them," said a man.

"I think the execution is tomorrow," said a woman.

"Where?"

"It's usually here in front of the courthouse."

"What time?"

"Someone said at nine."

"We must do something," Waya said. "We cannot let her die."

"I've got an idea," Tom said, "but we will need all of my sister's brain power to pull this off. We'll attack tomorrow during the execution, but we'll need more than Waya's bow and arrows."

Helene suggested, "Something like smoke bombs and Molotov cocktails?"

Tom replied, "Helene, you'll have to put the bombs together. What do we need?"

Helene thought back to the time at college when her girlfriend's car ran out of gas. She had used her smart phone to learn how to siphon gas out of a car's tank. Another time, some guys in a fraternity asked the "science major" if she could help them make a smoke bomb to throw at their rivals. She created a great bomb that cleared out the frat house.

"The first thing we'll need," she said, "is gasoline for the Molotov cocktails. That's not a problem if we can find a parked car with gas. Probably the military and police vehicles have gas, but that would not be the best choice. Tom, you and Waya need to find an abandoned refrigerator, take out the one-quarter-inch icemaker hose, and make a diagonal cut so it has a sharp point. Once you find a vehicle and insert the hose into the tank, it should take about four minutes to siphon enough gas for two large bottles.

"We passed what looked like a warehouse-supermarket on the way here. I'll barter my pistol for some saltpeter, baking soda, and sugar. We'll heat the mixture on our stove using our skillet and then pour the mixture into a tin foil ball and let it dry. Then all we need is a cigarette lighter to ignite the smoke bomb."

Tom and Waya located an old refrigerator in an abandoned section of southeast Atlanta. As they walked back towards city center, they spotted a police vehicle standing tireless on blocks next to the curb on a side street. The door was unlocked, so they opened the gas tank. Once they had access to the gas, they quickly siphoned out what they needed into two glass bottles. When they got back to the apartment, Helene was already cooking her smoke-bomb mixture in the skillet carefully placed on the wood stove.

Chapter 27
The Rescue

At eight-thirty the following morning, the three were in position, awaiting the execution. Waya leaned on the railing of the parking garage second deck, his bow and arrows at the ready. He would act first, and his arrows would signal the other two to launch their projectiles. From where he stood, Waya's arrows had a chance to hit any Black Sun executioner in the square. Helene stood east of the building with four smoke bombs hidden under her coat. She held a cigarette lighter in the palm of her hand. Tom took his position west of the entrance in front of the police station and near enough to the square to hear any words exchanged or orders given. Within target range were two wagons loaded with hay for the police horses. He had hidden the two Molotov cocktails under his jacket and a book of matches in his pocket.

A Black Sun captain appeared in the square. Dressed in a black leather aviator jacket adorned with Black Sun insignia and silver bars, he wore black pants, knee high black leather boots, dark sunglasses, and a black beret. Behind him in a procession walked first one soldier, three prisoners—imam, rabbi, and Mrs. Burk—and then two more soldiers. The group stopped in front of a stone wall situated next to the steps leading to the courthouse entrance.

The soldiers stood the three handcuffed prisoners in a line facing them. "I have one final request," Mrs. Burk said. "I would like to pray aloud. To do this, I need my hands free." The soldiers looked at the captain. He nodded his agreement and addressed Mrs. Burk, "Fine, but be quick about it. No more sermons."

Mrs. Burk bowed her head for a moment. Then she stood straight with her shoulders back. She looked at the soldiers and the crowd with her piercing, violet eyes, the same look she had given Tom and Helene when they first met. The sky above cleared for just a moment. Her voice shook but was audible to all the bystanders. "Father, forgive them for what they do. Include them in

Your grace."

"Enough," said the captain. Pulling out a paper document, he read the official charges. "These three criminals are guilty of undermining the law, aiding Islamic terrorists, supporting communists, defending homosexuals, speaking against Christianity, and, in one case..." he looked at Mrs. Burk, "...of blasphemy by preaching that we are all equal under God."

Folding the paper and shoving it into his jacket pocket, he shouted, "Prisoners, prepare to die."

Things moved quickly. Before Waya realized what was happening, the captain assigned one soldier to shoot each of the prisoners and quickly gave the signal by dropping his raised arm. Two shots rang out and the Imam and Rabbi fell to the ground before Waya could shoot his arrow. The third soldier's rifle jammed and Mrs. Burk stood, alive and untouched. The captain, deciding to do the job himself, pulled out his pistol and advanced, saying, "Your God of Love is dead and now, so are you. Die!"

Helene and Tom stood immobile, waiting for Waya, who knew he still had a chance to save Mrs. Burk. As the officer aimed, an arrow hit him in the buttocks, causing him to drop the pistol and fall sprawling on the ground.

Tom sprang into action, throwing his Molotov's at the two wagons full of hay, which caught fire. Panic ensued. Helene lit and launched her four smoke bombs in rapid succession. Blue smoke filled the air. From where Waya hid, it was impossible to see what was going on. The siblings melted into the crowd as confusion reigned. When the smoke cleared, Mrs. Burk had disappeared. Waya dropped behind the garage's upper story wall to avoid being seen. The Black Sun captain screamed from his prone position on the pavement, "Find her! Find that woman!"

The three friends had agreed to confirm they were surveillance-free before their rendezvous point at the Busy Bee Café on Trinity Avenue. It was a former soul-food restaurant with booths and a long, polished, rectangular wooden bar. Four metal stools with leather seats stood in a row beside it.

At eleven o'clock, the rendezvous hour, the place was filling with customers, but the bar stools remained empty. Tom arrived first, then Helene, then Waya. After they were seated on the stools, the three decided to move to an open booth where the noise of the other diners' conversations would provide enough sound masking to allow them to converse without being overheard.

Waya was the first to speak. "Was anyone followed?"

Tom shook his head. "I headed north toward the Peachtree Center, kept changing direction for several blocks, reversed, then doubled back here."

"I went east and south, and doubled back north," Helene said. "I did some window shopping to see if I could catch a follower's reflection in the windows like they do in movies I've seen, but I saw no one. Finally, I headed here as well."

Waya nodded. "I used some large shopping areas," he said, "then quiet side streets and a park. There was no one behind me, either. I think we're all good."

Then he whispered, "When the smoke cleared, she was gone. The captain was lying on the ground waiting for a stretcher and yelling at his men to go find her. In the panic and pandemonium, they didn't even know where to start looking. Too bad about the other two prisoners, though. We didn't save them."

Helene looked at the others and said softly, "We saved Mrs. Burk."

"There's just one thing," Waya continued. "When I took the shot, I prayed for the Great Spirit to guide my arm and make my arrow true. I knew Mrs. Burk's life depended on it. I had only one shot. Great Spirit answered me and said, 'I will guide your arrow to its target.' I guess Great Spirit didn't want me to kill him."

They ordered drinks and were still looking at the menu when the waiter returned with two coffees and a milk for Waya. Taking the drinks off the tray, he said, "The elderly woman at the bar didn't want to disturb you, so she asked me to give you this note." He handed Tom a folded piece of paper. Looking around to point her out, the waiter exclaimed, "Why, where is she? She was right over there." The three looked over at the bar. A couple were speaking quietly and looking intently into each other's eyes. She smiled and he nodded. A young, well-dressed blonde woman sat next to the couple, ordering coffee. The other stool was empty.

Tom opened the note. The paper had been folded, so the waiter could not see what had been written. He read it quickly and passed it to his sister, who read it and handed it to Waya. The note was no more than several short sentences. In spite of her age, they were written in a steady hand.

If you think God has forsaken us, think again. Never doubt his providence. He was there today because you three were there. You were His instruments of my salvation.

Waya, I'm so proud of you. You resisted the urge to kill. I know you could have shot that officer through the heart. Now he has a chance to live and turn his life around; be the person God made him to be. Bless you all. Go in God's grace.
    With Love,
    Mary Burk

Chapter 28
The Cruiser Olympia

Although they had already paid two weeks' rent, the three friends decided to leave Atlanta immediately. Learning that their contact at the tavern was under surveillance had spooked them. In addition, after their involvement in Mrs. Burk's escape, they thought the city was too dangerous for them. That night, they packed and left the next morning on the early train for Macon. Helene and Tom still had two gold pieces and Waya, two small diamonds. The trio paid for train passage to Macon with one of the gold pieces. Once in Macon, they discussed finding a ship that would sail much farther than the distance they had traveled from Henderson to Macon. They needed passage to South or

Central America. Brazil would be preferable, as that was supposedly where the Cross and Crescent was situated, far inland in the city of Brasilia.

But Helene had some doubts. As they began their search, Helene was hesitant and told the others, "I'm not sure we should leave the United States."

"Do you still think, after all that's happened, that our parents are still alive?" Tom asked.

"No. It's not that. I know they must be dead. Even if by some miracle they are alive, there is no way they could find us. It's just that maybe we should stay here and fight."

"Fight who, fight where?" Tom said. "The Resistance is dead. Easton is gone, Roanoke is gone, Blacksburg is gone, Atlanta is under Black Sun control, and we're on the run."

"I know," she said.

"You two need to make your own decision," Waya interrupted. "But I think if the three of us stay together, we can reach Brazil and contact these Cross and Crescent people. Maybe the rumor is true. Maybe they can change the world. If not, at least we will have tried."

After two days of searching, they found a ship, the former USS cruiser Olympia bound for Fortaleza,

Brazil. How the Olympia, a museum ship from the Philadelphia Sea Port Museum, came to be at dock in the Macon harbor was complicated. The captain, Rodney Shepfield, was a short, red-bearded man with curly hair and an auburn Imperial-style mustache. The bald spot on top of his head made him look like a medieval monk. The captain took his time telling his story, and the trio was forced to listen while they attempted to bargain for passage.

"Do you know who I am?" he asked the trio, and without waiting for an answer, proceeded to tell them. "I have been a historian, documentary film producer, yachtsman, and now captain of this ship, the Olympia. My girlfriend, Gaby, and I were visiting the Philadelphia Seaport Museum on the morning of Surge Saturday. We were among ten people touring the Olympia when the series of tsunamis hit the East Coast. The major surge in the mid-Atlantic not only destroyed Washington, D.C. but also put most of the state of Delaware under water. A second surge rolled across the Delaware Bay and up the Delaware River to the city of Philadelphia, which was permanently submerged.

"It was some kind of miracle. We escaped the wall of water that crashed over the city. I still don't know why or how we did it. It would seem impossible. But this ship has a long history. She once was Commodore Dewey's flagship during the victorious 1898 Battle of Manila Bay."

Shepfield then told then the rest of his story. Using his knowledge of the ship's abilities, he and his amateur crew managed to reach Charlotte, North Carolina. Despite the ship having only a token quantity of coal kept aboard for special outings, it was enough. In Charlotte, Shepfield found sufficient coal and a new volunteer crew and then sailed to Macon. At that point, the volunteers left the ship, having reached their destination. Shepfield needed another crew ready to travel a much larger distance and perhaps willing to take a one-way trip to South America.

Shepfield bartered some of the ship's old military equipment for more coal. He had most of the ship's silverware melted down and used the silver to hire a new crew and stock the ship with supplies. His girlfriend, Gaby, had family in Fortaleza, Brazil, and the two planned to sail to the northeast Brazilian coastal city. Life there would be easier as the climate was more hospitable, food was abundant, and, as far as they knew, there were no prevalent diseases that would destroy whole populations. However, they were uncertain if the city had survived.

"There must be something there," Held told the three travelers.

Smoothing his mustache with his fingers, Shepfield said that he would cut the price of their passage if they would work as crewmembers. He had already hired a crew of eleven for a ship that, in its heyday, had carried over 430 enlisted men and officers. He was not planning to fight anyone, and he figured a small number of crewmembers would do the trick.

Knowing they would need the gold pieces and at least a diamond in Brazil, the trio agreed to work as crew. As they were walking across the deck, Waya spotted something out of the corner of his eye. It was a crewmember putting a revolver in his belt, pulling his shirt over it, and then picking up a canvas bag.

"Hello," Waya said as he walked up to the crewmember and held out his right hand. When the man automatically stuck out his, Waya grabbed the hand and turned it backwards to the left and down, causing the man to fall. Within a second, Waya's knife was at his throat. Shepfield and the others stopped in amazement.

"What's going on Waya," Tom shouted.

Waya merely pulled the pistol from the man's belt and showed it to Shepfield and the others.

"Nicely done," Shepfield said. "Let's look at what he has in the bag."

When Shepfield opened the bag, some silver utensils from the ship's gallery fell out and clanked on the deck. Shepfield looked at Waya. "Please throw that weapon overboard and walk him off the ship."

Waya tossed the gun in the water and, holding the man's arm behind his back, did as Shepfield asked. He returned to the deck and held out his own knife, handle first.

"Keep your weapon," Shepfield said. "I need a good man like you. I have to watch this crew every second. All three of you are promoted to ship's officers."

He had a good feeling about the trio.

As they walked around the deck with Shepfield pointing at various equipment, the captain launched into a personal and historical monologue centering on his admiration for the Olympia. "You know that Surge Saturday, Gaby and I suddenly found ourselves in charge of this 1892, 344-foot steel cruiser, the oldest steel warship afloat. I believe the Olympia must have a charmed existence. She survived the Spanish American War, World War I, and then went on to provide humanitarian aid in the Adriatic during the Spanish flu epidemic of

1919. Now she survived a tsunami."

"So how did you come to be on the ship when the tsunami hit?" Helene asked. She soon regretted asking the question.

"That's a long story," Shepfield replied. "I have been an amateur military historian for years. My real work has focused on making film documentaries, specifically military history ones. Don't know if you've seen any of them? I did one about the Anglo-Zanzibar War of 1896 called The Forty-eight Minute War. I met Gaby when I was researching my second film on the War for Brazilian Independence. The war took place from 1822 to 1824 and ended with a Brazilian Empire and independence from Portugal. The material was great. It looked promising until the producers backed out, and I lost my funding. I completed it on my own but in a much-reduced fashion. We were at the Philadelphia Waterfront Museum because I planned to do a documentary about the Olympia and the Battle of Manila Bay. I wanted to reinforce details of the research I had developed on the cruiser's history and capabilities. That's why we were aboard that day, looking over the ship's interior and engine room."

"Wow," Helene replied, hoping that was the end of the monologue. But it was not.

Shepfield was a fount of knowledge about the ship's history. "After 27 years of service, which included two wars, the Olympia was mothballed until, in 1957, the U.S. Navy ceded title of the ship to the *Cruiser Olympia Association*. The association restored it to its 1898 condition, and, in 1960, moved it to the Philadelphia waterfront. In 2014, private donors provided the funds for extensive stabilization measures, including reinforcing the most deteriorated areas of the hull, expanding the alarm system, repairing the deck and ships rigging, and installing a network of bilge pumping stand pipes for damage control. In 2030 and 2040, the ship was certified seaworthy. Of course, it was not modernized as it remained a museum ship."

As no one had the courage to stop him, Shepfield continued his somniferous monologue. "She is a fantastic craft designed during the New 'Steel Navy' era of American history and is one of the first ships to be equipped with refrigeration, a radio communications system, and one of the first to use steam for a host of tasks. Three coal-fired cylindrical boilers supply steam to a pair of vertical triple expansion engines, which power the ship. Two smokestacks release the exhaust. Her length is 344 feet, and her width is fifty-three feet, with a draft of twenty-one feet, six inches from the waterline to the bottom of the hull. Her top speed is twenty-three knots per hour."

Mesmerized by the extent of his own knowledge, Shepfield seemed unaware of his audience's waning interest. They couldn't have cared less about the ship's length, height, speed or capabilities.

"Does she have active defenses?" Tom asked. "I mean, can we defend ourselves if we have to?" His sister shot him a look that told him exactly what she thought of his encouraging the man to keep talking.

Shepfield, rolling along like a freight train, continued with a full description of the ship's armaments. "The navy replaced twin turret guns with open gun platforms of higher caliber. Unfortunately, these fourteen and six-pounders are no longer functional. I recently found ammunition for the two older 1911-made Gatling guns. They work like a charm."

Anxious to get away, the three told Shepfield they would come back the next day ready to bunk on board and help run the ship. "That's great," he said. "The other ten are already on board, and I'll introduce you to my girlfriend, Gaby, who will be the ship's cook."

Once away from the ship, the three travelers discussed

their plans. "He seems a bit quirky," Helene said. "Do you guys trust him?"

Tom replied, "He appears to know a lot about the cruiser. I hope it is seaworthy. They reviewed the ship for seaworthiness ten years ago."

Helene added, "He made it to Charlotte and then here, so he must know what he is doing, and the boat seems to stay afloat. Also, he's got a crew and coal. I believe he can make Brazil. He probably plans to stop in the Caribbean to replenish his supplies. As for the crew's reliability, especially after the earlier incident, there is no telling…"

Waya broke in, "We don't have a choice. No other ships are sailing for Central America or Brazil. We can't stay here. We must find people who can help us fix the sky."

"Plus, he has ammunition for the Gatling guns in case we meet Black Sun or whomever," Tom said.

Chapter 29
Welcome Aboard

The next morning, the three walked up the gangplank, carrying what small possessions they had. Shepfield and Gaby were there to greet them. Gaby, an Afro-Brazilian with a somewhat dark complexion, was what the Brazilians call a *morena*. She had turquoise eyes with blonde hair. Her ancestors had arrived in Brazil from Africa on the slave boats that docked in Bahia. The blonde, blue, and green-eyed Portuguese colonists first bedded the slaves and later intermarried with the light and dark-skinned, brown-eyed Africans. Gaby had inherited the eyes and hair of her Portuguese forbearers and the light brown skin of her African forefathers. All in all, an amazing mixture.

As they descended the stairs from the glass-enclosed hatch, they found themselves transported to a far-away time. The officers' quarters lay to the left and right of an ornate wood-paneled hallway. The outside cabins all had windows and were fitted with oak dressers, desks, and small wooden beds. Past the officers' quarters on the upper deck was an elaborate dining hall. The room had vintage detailing on all the oak panels. The floors, like the hallway, were light cedar. There was a mahogany cabinet with a 1900s Victrola on top. The room was lit with oil lamps and, from the large bay window, the officers had a good view of the sea. There were six chairs and a large dining table, all made of white oak. The table was set with four place settings of white china and real, not plated, silver knives, forks, and spoons. An antique Georgian Welsh mahogany grandfather clock sat in the corner. With gold dials, brass-weighted pendulum, polished wood cabinet, and a glazed glass front door, it was a sight to see. On the top, three gold balls supported gold-plated eagle finials. The clock still chimed out the hour. A small kitchen sat off to the side, accessible through two swinging doors.

"I believe we have stepped back into the past," Helene said. "All you guys need are navy uniforms from that period. Just like the mock-up officer's attire on display in one of the lounges. You would look handsome in blue velvet with a blue-visored cap with the silver letters U.S.N."

"I think we've time traveled," Tom agreed. "Things were much simpler then. The U.S. navy reigned supreme and there was no Black Sun."

Shepfield led them down a ladder to the lower deck. Half of this deck was devoted to the engines and boiler room. The other half consisted of the crew's quarters. They slept on hammocks in a group sleeping area, but the wood paneling on the room's walls was tastefully done. The crew ate in a larger dining hall with an adjoining kitchen. The ten crew members had staked out their sleeping positions and were currently playing cards on a small wooden gaming table in a less ornate parlor. Shepfield left the introductions for later and returned with the trio to the officer's deck, where he told them to choose their rooms. He and Gaby, of course, had already taken the captain's stateroom.

That night Waya, Tom, and Helene dined with Gaby and Shepfield. Gaby first fed the crew of ten in the crew's dining hall then returned upstairs to serve the five of them. She had prepared all the food in the small officers' kitchen. Earlier in the day, they had seen large bags of rice and potatoes in the downstairs galley. Meat was more difficult to come by unless salted or smoked, but some of each hung from hooks in the galley below. Sacks of black beans and canned fruit were stacked in the corner of the storeroom.

Gaby prepared a Brazilian *feijoada* with rice and black beans and small pieces of smoked *linguica* sausage and salt pork. She served the feijoada with *farofa*, a flour mixed with onions. The smell of the dish when she spooned it over white rice made their mouths water. The odor of garlic, cloves, bay leaves, and onion permeated the room. Gaby apologized for the lack of collard greens, but they had proven impossible to find. She placed a canned pineapple slice on the side of each dish. Helene and Tom could not remember ever having had such quality food except once in a restaurant in Richmond, Virginia, many years before. Even Waya, a vegetarian who ate around his pieces of pork, seemed to enjoy the meal.

During dinner, the conversation switched quickly from topic to topic. Gaby spoke about her childhood in northeastern Brazil. Shepfield told them, "Gaby and I met when I was researching my second film, the one on the war for Brazilian independence. She helped me translate documents from Portuguese and, as I mentioned, was deeply involved in my later research on the Olympia's history. We fell in love, and we were thinking about getting married. Surge Saturday interrupted this, but we're hoping to find a home in Brazil. Philadelphia to Charlotte was an adventure, but the trip to Brazil will be even more daring. But we like adventure, don't we, meu amor?"

Gaby simply smiled in response.

Helene discussed their own experiences. "We were going to drive from Easton, Pennsylvania, where I was in school, to Washington, D.C. to see our parents for Labor Day. After Surge Saturday, and realizing we could starve at Lafayette College, we hitchhiked down route 81, along the Blue Ridge. At a rest stop along the highway, Waya saved us from some criminals. We teamed up then traveled to Ashville and southeast to Greenville, South Carolina. There, we took a boat to Macon-Atlanta, and here we are."

Helene purposely left out their arrest and deliverance in Roanoke, their fight on the side of the resistance in Blacksburg, their meeting with Mrs. Burk, their role in saving her, and the reason they had to leave Atlanta.

"We simply wanted to go to South America to escape the year-round winter cold," Tom said, "and outbreaks of disease in Atlanta. We thought we could seek refuge somewhere below the equator."

Waya remained silent, except to say that he was Waya of the Cherokee born in the mountains of North Carolina.

It was obvious that Shepfield and Gaby were very much in love. The looks they gave each other when they thought no one was watching, the manner in which he caressed her shoulder, the way she called him *meu amor*, and he called her *minha flor*, were all signs of their affection. They were a perfect example of the old saying, "opposites attract." Shepfield with his red hair, fair skin, British heritage, and Gaby, a tanned *morena* with blonde hair. Gaby was like some wild orchid, beautiful and exotic. Her cooking showed her passion for life. Shepfield appeared academic and somewhat sedentary, with a proclivity for research. His passion for Gaby, his willingness to take control of the Olympia, and his will to survive hinted at something deeper in the man. Perhaps he was more than he seemed to be. Tom remembered a saying of his grandmother's: "Still waters run deep."

To test the waters and see if they could trust Shepfield with their secrets, Tom asked, "Why are you two taking the immense risk of sailing to Brazil?"

"As I mentioned, we wanted a new life," Shepfield replied. "Since Black Sun took over and with the problems of food shortages, outbreaks of disease, and lack of employment, we felt we needed to leave America. Gaby thought it was best if we went to her relatives in Brazil. Now we're not sure. Gaby heard on the ship's radio that a group called the Golden Day, with a similar ideology to Black Sun, has taken over the eastern seaboard of Brazil and established a new capital in São Paulo. Brasilia, the former Brazilian capital, is too far from the coast. Golden Day has also taken over the planned city of Curitiba to the south of Sao Paulo in the state of Paraná. I hope we're not trading one nightmare for another."

The siblings remained silent. Though they felt Shepfield might be sympathetic to their and Waya's quest, they did not dare risk revealing their plans. Especially after Shepfield ended the conversation by speaking of those who opposed Black Sun as idealists. "You got to protect yourself first. Crusades against evil are great in romance novels, but many crusaders die young and with nothing to show for their effort."

Shepfield decided that he, Tom, and Waya would divide the night's watch. "There should not be a lot of nautical traffic," Shepfield said, "but we will soon be going out into open sea with its storms and possible risk of pirates." Shepfield took the first three hours, Waya next, and Tom the last. They would work on a daily schedule when they had time the next day.

Chapter 30
South to the Caribbean

Tom was still on watch when, at seven a.m. sharp, Shepfield arrived on the upper deck and took his position in the Captain's chair. The crew had been up for two hours and the ship was ready to move under full steam. Gaby had fed them eggs and salted bacon for breakfast. Waya was walking around the ship, taking in the activities of the crew. Helene was still asleep.

At dinner the night before, Shepfield told the travelers he had found a navigational chart of what had been the Caribbean, Central, and South America. He used the ship's shortwave radio to contact radio operators in various port cities in Central and South America to discover ports that still existed, those which had not been swallowed by the sea.

Shepfield had told them, "From what I've heard, only the higher elevations of Cuba, Dominican Republic, and some mountainous regions in Central America have survived the flood. My contacts say that a large inland sea covers much of the Amazon, including the former Brazilian state of Amapa and a large part of the state of Pará. Pará's capital, the port of Belém, is under water. The countries of Suriname, Guyana, and the French overseas territory of Guiana still exist, but I'm not sure about their capitals. They were all coastal cities. We will need to put in for supplies before reaching Fortaleza, Ceará, where Gaby's family live.

"Unlike the U.S. where the average water level rose by 350 feet, according to what I hear, the highest sea level increase in Latin America and the Caribbean was around 300 feet. If you want to travel farther south past Fortaleza, be aware that Bahia, Rio, Santos, Porto Alegre, Montevideo, and Buenos Aires are all under water. Asuncion, Paraguay has become a new port on a second inland sea that now runs over parts of Uruguay and Argentina. However, the cities of São Paulo and Curitiba both survived, and I've heard radio operators from there reaching out."

That morning, Tom watched Shepfield guide the ship out of the harbor and onto the open sea. The captain motioned for Tom to join him. "Today, you'll watch everything I do so that you can pilot the ship yourself and teach the other two.

"Next stop Havana, or what's left of it. Then Santo Domingo, and then we can put in somewhere close to Paramaribo or Cayenne before sailing to Fortaleza. The highest part of the Fortaleza, where the cathedral sat, was only 69 feet above sea level. I could not raise anyone on the shortwave. However, fifty-four kilometers southwest is the small town of Pacajùs which survived the tsunami and the subsequent rise in water level. I heard a shortwave station broadcasting from that city."

Tom hoped Shepfield knew what he was doing.

Chapter 31
Cuba

Following three days of smooth sailing, the Olympia reached the island of Cuba. The crew was surprised that they had not faced any storms, but they had been lucky. By then, the three travelers had begun to learn the basics of piloting the ship. Havana, at its highest level, had been only194 feet above sea level. The whole city, including the old colonial area, was now submerged and even the top spire of the historic cathedral was below the depths.

Shepfield wanted to avoid the potential risks involved in docking above a submerged city and decided to sail around the 780-mile-long island to reach Guantanamo Bay. It would take at least a day to reach Caimanera-

Guantanamo, a new southeastern city. As they rounded the southeastern tip, they realized that the Archipelagos Jardines de la Reina, Canarreos, and Los Colorados had disappeared. However, the historic city of Guantanamo, located in the foothills of the Sierra Maestra, still existed. It was originally fifteen miles from both the eastern end of Guantanamo bay and the old port of Caimanera. The water had pushed through Caimanera up to the foothills to an area just below historic Guantanamo. The city was now a port.

The former Naval Station Guantanamo Bay, previously referred to as Gitmo, had been taken over by the Cubans in 2030 and made into a vacation paradise. This piece of land stood at only 75 feet above sea level before the surge. The town had not withstood the waters' rise. The hotels, stores, and shops, along with the historic prison and the ghosts of the terrorists detained there, were now submerged under the sea.

The new capital of Cuba was Bayamo. Though less known than the now-submerged cities of Havana and Santiago, Bayamo was much older. Built in the high Sierra Maestra Mountains, its location had provided a sanctuary from the sea. The citizens survived through a newly developed fishing industry based out of the new

Caimanera-Guantanamo. Fishermen sold their catch to transportation men who brought the seafood by donkey up the mountains from the bay. On their return, they carried rice, potatoes, fruit, and beef back down to the port.

The Olympia arrived in Guantanamo Bay on the morning of her fifth day at sea. "We are not staying long," Shepfield told the crew. "No one goes ashore. Tom and I will go alone. We'll get some fresh fruit, water, fish, and coal, or wood if they don't have coal. We've got a functioning refrigerator, and we can salt the fish that won't fit."

At ten that morning, the two took the dinghy ashore, docked at the wharf, and entered the main town square just off the harbor. An old, dilapidated church stood at one corner of the square. On the other side was a stone building, covered in vines and moss. It had been both the post office and town hall but was now abandoned. Near the Plaza de la Revolución, sat an open grassy field filled with waste and the aroma of rotting food. The slightly sweet odor of rancid meat mixed with the sour smell of rotten fish and vegetables. A mass of poorly dressed locals crowded around some stalls and called out what they need and what they could barter in return. Shepfield and Tom found vendors who sold rice, potatoes, beans, oranges, tacos, and fish. Shepfield's Portuñol and Tom's acceptable French allowed them to purchase what they needed using a sort of pidgin Spanish.

Their business concluded, Tom and Shepfield accompanied Matheus, one of the chief vendors, to a local restaurant called the Girasol to celebrate the transactions. Matheus, a dark-skinned fellow dressed in a colorful guayabera and a straw hat, spent most of his days playing dominos on the square when not selling his wares. He spoke few words of English, but the lunch was more about the camaraderie and food than in-depth conversation. The three sat on the restaurant's balcony under a sun umbrella and ate *ropa vieja*, a traditional Cuban dish made of stewed shredded beef with onions, tomatoes, garlic, and wine and served with rice and black beans. Matheus had suggested the dish, which was excellent, and Tom was disappointed that Helene was not there to share the delicious meal.

Lunch finished, Matheus introduced them to a friend who had wood for sale. When done with all their purchases, they paid with the silver Shepfield had kept on board. They also hired some locals to transport the wood along with the sacks of rice, beans, and oranges to the dock. Once there, it took three trips with the dinghy to get all the supplies, including the wood, back to the ship. When all was on board, Shepfield was ready to depart. The crew then informed him that a crewmember named Martins was missing.

Martins had disappeared for several hours shortly after Tom and Shepfield left for the port of Caimanera-Guantanamo. A small sailboat met him and took him ashore. When Martins finally returned to the ship, the captain, who was impatiently waiting, called for an explanation. Martins replied that he had used the ship's radio to contact a marijuana planter he knew of and whose contact info he had been given in Atlanta. He brought back a load, which he shared with the crew. Shepfield was unhappy that Martins had disobeyed his direct order, but the crew heartily approved of the action. The captain did not want to challenge Martins directly in front of the crew and, as he was not sure of their loyalty, simply ordered the men to haul anchor and set sail for the Dominican Republic that afternoon.

Chapter 32
Santo Domingo

Quisqueya, mother of all lands in the Taino dialect, now the Dominican Republic, had fared better than its island neighbor, Haiti. The former French half of the dual-country island was destroyed by a tsunami. Shepfield planned to dock near the town of Bani, on the Dominican side. Bani, the word for abundant water in Taino, proved to be a prophetic name. Formerly in the foothills of the country's central mountains, it was now a port city on the coast. It replaced Santo Domingo, which had sunk after the rise in sea level, as the capital.

The Dominican Republic now resembled the country of Norway except that in Dominican Republic, the fjords were made by the rising sea. These new bodies of water divided the four mountain ranges: the Cordillera Central above Santo Domingo, the Cordillera Oriental to the southeast, the Cordillera Septrioal to the northeast, and the Sierra de Bahoruco to the southwest. The sea had swallowed Lake Enriquillo and the Ozania River.

Rounding the southeast tip of the island, the Olympia hugged the coast, moving between the mainland and Soana Island. Soana, fifteen-and-a-half miles in length, was a former tourist paradise filled with rare animals and thick jungle. After the flood, only certain high areas remained, but these were still accessible from the coast by catamarans or "Beachcats." These boats consisted of a mast with a main sail and jib and two hulls. Made of the most developed fiberglass components and known for their speed and stability, they usually ran around twenty-three feet in length.

Out of nowhere, three Beachcats appeared behind the Olympia. They must have been hidden behind what was left of the small island and closed quickly on the cruiser. All three were flying some kind of black flag. Shepfield pulled out a pair of binoculars and squinted through them. The nearest Beachcat appeared to be flying the skull and crossbones. "Oh shit, oh shit," yelled Shepfield, sounding like he was out of breath. "This does not look good. Looks like pirates. We may not be able to outrun them. I hope we can fight them off."

"What do you want us to do?" Tom said.

When Beachcats grew closer, Shepfield followed them with his binoculars. The captain of the lagging catamaran wore a tight-fitting black body t-shirt, black shorts, and a black beret. His ebony arms and legs glistened with sweat. Shepfield could make out his white teeth and a malicious smile. With his dark skin, black pencil-style mustache, and black sunglasses, the captain resembled a historic Somalian pirate, one of those who had sailed off the coast of Africa. He carried what appeared to be an old AK or similar machine-gun and he waved his hands to the three crews, as if he were egging the boats forward.

"Sound the alarm," Shepfield told Tom. "All hands on deck."

Waya and Helene ran to the steps, climbed to the control cabin, and joined Shepfield and Tom.

"What's going on?" shouted Helene.

"Three pirate boats astern, closing quickly," the captain responded.

Rapid machine-gun fire erupted from the first small craft and caused Shepfield to shout, "Man the Gatling guns." Two of the crew ran to the forward gun and another two to the aft. One crewmember began hand cranking the weapon while his partner controlled the hopper, which dropped the cartridges into the carrier. The ten-barreled guns rotated and fired. The aft gun hit one of the three approaching boats and tore it to pieces. The sailboat drifted aimlessly to the side, pushed only by the wind. But Gatling guns are always sensitive to jamming. The aft guns' barrels heated up and began to glow red. The gun jammed. Machine-gun fire from the second catamaran strafed the deck. The balding captain and the trio to dropped to the ground.

Shepfield dove for the controls. He brought the ship about, bringing the forward gun into position to fire. It stopped the second catamaran by cutting through its sails and hitting all the crew members. However, machine-gun fire from the pirate command boat struck the two forward gunners. Their gun fell silent.

Shepfield and the trio were at a loss. Even if they had handguns in addition to the Gatling guns, they would have been no match for the machine guns carried by the pirates. As the remaining catamaran moved close, the captain cut the ship's motors. "We can't outrun them," he said.

"You're not giving up without a fight?" Helene said. "They'll probably kill us all."

The redheaded captain put his finger to his lips and motioned for her to be silent. He quickly descended to the upper deck. The three followed him and watched him avoid enemy fire by crawling toward an oar box. Reaching in, he pulled out three old hand grenades and handed one to Waya, one to Tom, and the third to Helene. "There is only one grenade left. I am going to stand up and pretend to surrender. When I drop my white handkerchief, the three of you toss the grenades."

The catamaran pulled up and its five-member crew pointed their AKs at the deck of the Olympia. The Haitian captain yelled, "Get manman ou," which sounded a lot like, "go do something to your mother."

Seeing Shepfield and the trio on deck, the Haitian continued in creole. "Djol kaka, vin isit la." Then, in more traditional French, "Bouche de merde, venez ici. Rendez-vous où mourir."

Tom loosely translated for Shepfield. "He said, 'Shit-mouth, surrender now or die.'"

The Olympia's captain stood up and waved his white handkerchief, then yelled, "We surrender. Come aboard."

As if a wisp of wind had hit the handkerchief, Shepfield

let it drop and dove after it. Machine gun fire followed his diving body. The trio tossed their grenades at the pirate boat. Two hit the sides of the boat, splashing water and causing damage to the side hulls. Waya's grenade hit dead center, striking several pirates. A nine-millimeter pistol suddenly appeared in Shepfield's hand. He stood up and, as calmly as if he had been shooting targets at a practice range, he shot the pirates who were still standing.

Helene looked at him with amazement. "Where the hell did you learn to shoot like that?"

The redheaded filmmaker just smiled and smoothed his auburn mustache. "When I was working on one of my documentaries, I decided to take shooting lessons and continued to spend time at the range until several months ago. As for the 9mm, with the unknown crew we have below, I wouldn't trust my life and Gaby's to chance."

There was a lot more to Shepfield than Helene had originally imagined.

Chapter 33
The Arawak

After the incident with the pirates, Shepfield decided they would not put into port at Bani. He was not sure if more trouble awaited them there, so instead they sailed for the coast of Venezuela. Caracas was under water and they sailed on.

Five days after leaving Cuba and following the coast of Venezuela and Guyana, they arrived at a spot near the former city of Paramaribo, Belize. Where the city should have stood, there was nothing. They dropped anchor and waited for morning. The next day, Shepfield chose to sail further south to Cayenne, the capital of French Guiana. Early that morning, when they arrived, it was evident that

Cayenne had also disappeared underneath the water. The captain expressed his doubts aloud. "Half the population of French Guiana lived in Cayenne. I wondered if they had had time to flee farther inland and take shelter in the rain forests of the Tumak Humak Mountains."

Where the mouth of the Oyapock River should have been, there was a large bay but no river. On one bank, now a coastline, was French Guiana and on the other side was Brazil. From the middle of the sea, the ship could see neither coast. To make it worse, a fog rolled in. Vision was almost impossible.

Shepfield ordered, "We'll wait out the fog inside the bay in calmer waters, but I don't want to get too close to either coast in this fog."

Fortunately, the sea remained calm. The trio met on deck to discuss their next steps. "We need to be careful. Both capital cities are gone," Tom opined. "We do need to take on water so it is best that we sail inland. But we don't know how deep the water will run."

Helene agreed. "I don't know how far the sea has moved inland. Obviously, the river is now a bay and could lead to an inland sea or just the mouth of the river, but farther inland from where it was. At some point, the river will narrow."

Shepfield, who had joined them, said. "We need to get supplies before sailing down to Fortaleza since we don't know what we'll find there. Tomorrow, we'll sail inland to the town of Saint Georges. According to my research, it's located on the French side of the Oyapock River. It's connected to Brazil by a two-towered high suspension bridge. There is supposed to be a French Foreign Legion base there where we can get supplies and information."

The next morning, with the fog lifted, Shepfield gave the command. "We sail inland."

After two hours of sailing, all they saw was the inland sea or enlarged bay with neither coast in view. There was no river, no bridge, and no Saint Georges. The French city was now submerged under the inland sea. A disappointed Shepfield told the crew, "We'll have to sail even farther inland until we find a town that is still intact. This sea-river appears to be deep enough, but we'll have to be very careful and maybe try to take some soundings of the river's depth."

An hour later, they arrived at the location where, according to Shepfield's map, the town of Camopi was supposed to be found.

Where the city should have been, there was only water for miles on either side. Everything was gone. The trio, along with Shepfield and Gaby, were shocked. They seemed to be out of options.

"What do we do now?" Helene asked.

"The topography of the area shows an elevation to the north," Shepfield said. "I suggest we sail in that direction."

"Let's try," Waya said. "I agree with the captain."

At the northern side of the sea, they found the village of Bienvenu. This small village had survived the rise in water level. The Olympia dropped anchor off Bienvenu, and Shepfield assembled the crew.

"I don't want to venture farther inland," he said. "The sea-river may get shallow after this. Let's see if we can get some supplies here. We'll send a landing party ashore."

The landing party, composed of Waya, Tom, Gaby, and Helene, set out in the skiff, leaving the crew to take care of the ship. Shepfield remained on board. He was afraid the crew might sail away without them. When the skiff had gotten halfway to shore, a large dugout made of a single tree met them. It looked like half the village was in the boat. The Indians motioned for them to follow the canoe back to their village.

❦❦❦

A dark-skinned woman of impressive stature and bearing met them when they docked. Her long, coarse, black hair fell below her shoulders to the middle of her back. Her pupils were dark brown with substantial white around the brown. She was bare breasted and wore large earrings that hung from her ears like golden grapes. Her nose, broad and somewhat flat, contributed to her magnificence. High cheekbones and white teeth framed by full, sensual lips completed her description.

"My name is Shoko Laliwa, and I am the *caique* or leader of this village. We are called the Lokono or Arawak," she said in Portuguese. "My name means little yellow butterfly, but you can call me Marian. I was named after Princess Marian, who was chieftess of the Eagle Clan in the late 1800s."

Gaby quickly translated her words into English for the benefit of her companions.

Marian wanted to know why they were there and what they wanted. Gaby explained that they needed provisions and could trade for them with items from their stock of rice, beans, and dried meat. In return the chieftess offered fresh fish, fruit, and vegetables. She told them her tribe were farmers, hunters, and fishermen. Since the day of the great flood, they spent a lot more time fishing as the fresh water river had turned salty and brought ocean fish to this new inland sea. "Farther inland," she said, "the water is fresh as the ocean could not reverse the river's flow. But that is many miles past our village."

After the initial greetings, Marian invited them to dine at her home. As they entered the village, she explained how things worked. "I am the caique, so I assign daily work, make sure everyone gets an equal share, and decide who farms, who fishes, and who hunts."

They moved into an open area, a level courtyard in which children were playing soccer and women cooking various foods, from fish to vegetables. At one end of the courtyard was a large circular building with wooden poles, *bohios*, Marian said. The roof was made of woven straw and palm leaves. Looking inside, the visitors could see hammocks of cotton and sleeping mats made of banana leaves. At the other end of the village was a rectangular house with a porch in front. "That's my house where we will dine," Marian told them.

While they enjoyed a meal of fresh-cooked fish and vegetables, Marian spoke of her tribe and her role as leader. Gaby translated for her from Portuguese to English. "I was educated in Manaus and that is why I speak Portuguese," she said. "I also learned French, as we live in a French overseas department, but I have forgotten a lot. I speak a few words of English but my English is not so good."

"Domage," said Tom. "Je parle un petit peut du français et ma sœur parle aussi."

Marian smiled and said in French, "I think I should continue to speak Portuguese as it is easier for me than French and your Brazilian friend can translate. Let me tell you about our history."

"The Arawak tribe was here in 1496 when the Spanish arrived. They fought the Spanish but then allied with them against the British, Dutch, and Caribs or Creoles. The tribe originally lived on the coast, but we were pushed further inland. We retreated into the rain forest. Some of our tribe lived near Camopi until the sky fell and the waters rose. They came here to join us. We are safe, but our river has become an ocean."

"What was Camopi like?" Helene asked.

"Camopi had a lengthy history starting with the Jesuits in 1738. It was the first settlement on the Oyapock. Different Indian tribes lived here and disputed the territory. In the eighties, gold was discovered which brought French miners. More recently, the Indians of my tribe began to farm the land around Camopi on small agricultural plots. With the great flood, they have now disappeared.

"Before we trade," Marian said, "I would like you

to take part in a ceremony of friendship. We will pass around a cigar called Yoni in my language. It is made of tobacco grown here. Since it is a religious ceremony, using a manufactured cigar would be sacrilege. This one is hand-rolled. I would like to explain the meaning of the ceremony. We believe that we all come from the spirit world and are by nature good, generous and belong to one family. The spirits come to the physical world from their true place of origin, the real world, the spirit world. Our shaman, the man passing the cigar, is our portal to the spirit world. We live separate and try to keep the ancient ways."

Waya spoke up and told Gaby, "Please tell her that I am Waya of the Cherokee, an old and powerful tribe from North America. We serve the Creator Spirit who made all men one with the earth and all living things. My ancestors predicted these times of flood and destruction. Tell her that we three are on a mission to open the windows of heaven, so the sun will shine bright once more."

After Gaby translated what Waya had said, Marian replied, "Welcome, Waya of the Cherokee. Your mission is important to all our tribes. We have fought long and hard to protect our forest from the greed that has brought doom upon this world. We wish you success in your mission. Where will you go?"

Waya replied, "Tell her we will go to Brasilia to find a group of shamans who are praying to save this world and who talk directly with the Great Spirit."

"I know this place. It is the capital of Brazil. But you will have a long journey."

Gaby replied in Portuguese, "Brasilia is no longer the capital. Now the capital is in São Paulo. My fiancée and I will take them to Fortaleza on our ship. Then they must get to São Paulo and begin the long trek to Brasilia."

Directing her question to the trio, Gaby said in English, "You are really going to Brasilia on a quest to save the world from Black Sun and their allies? Why didn't you tell Shepfield? He is not fond of Black Sun either. We will do our best to help you get to São Paulo."

That night they returned to the ship and told Shepfield all that had happened during their visit ashore. When Gaby mentioned the trio's quest, Shepfield was offended that they had not trusted him with their true goal. "We'll take the boat to Fortaleza," he said. "I plan to drop anchor off the coast there. If, as I suspect, nothing is there, we will find Pacajùs or whatever port we can and help you arrange a boat to São Paulo. Are you sure you want to go south? It will be dangerous. If we can find them, Gaby's relatives may have contacts that can be useful."

The next morning, several canoes arrived laden with fresh fish and vegetables and took away dried pork, salted bacon, beans, and sacks of rice. As they weighed anchor, Marian waved from her dugout and called out in Portuguese, "May we meet again in the spirit world from which we all come."

Chapter 34
Fortaleza- Pacajùs

The city of Fortaleza, with its three-storied Civic Center, Metropolitan Cathedral with its two-towers and stained-glass windows, and the magnificent Fortress of Our Lady of Assumption, was the fifth largest city in Brazil. Everything had disappeared under the sea. Gone were the famous water park, Beach Park, Red Cliffs, and labyrinths of colored sand dunes of the Morro Branco. Most of the nearby towns had also disappeared. All the travelers saw was endless water that had encroached on the coastline. The coast was lost in mist. Fifty-four kilometers southwest from Fortaleza, the city of Pacajùs had survived. It had become the new state capital, and a port city located at the northeast corner of the former

Lake Pacajùs. The lake, swallowed by the ocean, was now part of a large bay.

Shepfield steered the ship toward the harbor and dropped anchor.

The captain was about to call a meeting with the crew to discuss disembarking when he saw them descending single file to the lower deck. Following Martins, they all headed toward the crew's dining hall. Something seemed wrong, so Shepfield quietly shadowed them. When the crew reached their destination, Martins asked them to find seats as he had a proposal for them. The captain surreptitiously entered a side door to the crew's kitchen and hid behind the door to the adjoining dining hall.

Martins began, "Only one or two of you know that I work with Black Sun. The Black Sun Party and their new government are what have saved what is left of the United States. They have been what has stood between order and anarchy, stability and terrorism. They put me aboard this vessel to make contact with Golden Day, a similar group here in Brazil. When our new three officers signed on in Macon-Atlanta, I was a bit suspicious and met with my Black Sun Government contact just before we left. He told me he'd check them out and that I should contact him by radio from wherever the ship first docked.

"In Cuba, I didn't go ashore only for the weed. That was just a cover. I found a shortwave radio operator in Caimanera and reached out to my Atlanta contact. He informed me that the three strangers were the same people who foiled an execution in Atlanta. Two of them might even be Cross and Crescent, a terrorist group opposed to Black Sun's government.

Shepfield listened in amazement. *He had never liked or trusted Martins. But working for Black Sun? He never would have believed the government's power extended so far. His three friends must be pretty important if Black Sun would send someone to follow them to Brazil. What did Black Sun want with them?* He shut off his thoughts and listened.

"My contact issued me a radio call sign and a frequency that I could use to reach Golden Day. I reached out to the Fortaleza organization on the ship's radio this morning. They told me to keep them apprised of the suspects' activities. They want to capture them at some point and question them about their contacts in Brazil. The three must have someone who will help them, and Golden Day wants the terrorist network eliminated.

"My idea is to capture them ourselves and hand them over to Golden Day for a reward. We should be able to overwhelm two men, the Indian, and two women. If we let them leave, Golden Day will probably arrest them at some point, and we won't get any reward."

Martins waited for their response. One of the men, Jenkins, a tall bearded pot-smoking crewmember who spent a lot of time with Martins, jumped up shouting, "Count me in." The others followed suit.

Pulling out a revolver, Martins told the crew, "Grab whatever serves as a weapon and follow me. We'll surprise them. I don't want to use the Gatling guns as they will not be effective at close range and might damage the ship."

Some of the crew began grabbing coal shovels, others seized lead pipes or iron wrenches. Still others pulled out knives they had hidden in their clothing.

Shepfield backed out of the kitchen and hurriedly climbed to the first deck. He found Gaby in the kitchen and told her to run and find the three travelers. He went to the captain's cabin, retrieved his pistol, and snatched the remaining hand grenade he had stored there after the fight with the pirates.

Gaby returned with Helene, Waya, and Tom running behind her. Shepfield related what he had overheard. "You three need to get into the skiff and head for land. Gaby, you go, too. They will need someone who speaks Portuguese..." He stopped abruptly, not wanting to alarm her.

"But what about you, *amor*?" Gaby said. "What do you plan to do? Eu não vou sem você."

Shepfield answered, "Minha flor, you have to go. Você sabe, I'm no hero. I'll just stop them, and then I'll be right behind you." Shepfield looked at Helene, and she realized he wanted Gaby out of earshot. He repeated, "Gaby, vai amor. Help Helene and Waya with the dinghy. Now!"

Helene grabbed Gaby's arm and said, "Come with me. Everything will be fine. Tom can stay with Shepfield."

With the others preparing to lower the skiff and thus out of earshot, Shepfield turned to Tom. "Help them lower the boat and wait in the water beside the ship. If I don't appear on deck in a five minutes, leave. Make sure Gaby doesn't go ballistic. Take care of her."

"You don't have to do this on your own," Tom replied, "I'll stay and fight by your side."

"The Indian is a courageous soul, but you need to be with them, Tom," Shepfield replied. "Now go help them. It's the way it has to be. I'll be right along."

Tom ran toward the group lowering the skiff. Once the dinghy with three passengers was in the water, Waya, who had remained on board to make sure it lowered correctly, shimmied down the rope to join them. They all looked up at the deck, anxiously waiting for Shepfield to appear.

Meanwhile, Shepfield returned to the top of the main stairs. Two of the crew had already reached the upper deck and as they approached, he fired his pistol, quickly killing them before they could attack. Martins, however, had arrived via another stairway located to Shepfield's rear. He aimed his revolver and shot, hitting Shepfield in the shoulder. The remaining crew members, carrying shovels and knives, exited the stairway. They rushed Shepfield, who was busy returning Martins' fire. Seeing he did not have time to reload and fire, Shepfield pulled the grenade pin, counted, tossed it at them, and dove behind the cabin. The grenade killed all three crew members immediately.

While Shepfield was lying on the ground with his ears ringing from the grenade blast, Martins walked up from behind and shot him in the back of the head. Blood running from the bullet hole, Shepfield fell back, dying. *It's not supposed to happen this way. I'm no hero.*

In the blink of an eye, without forethought, Rodney Shepfield, unknown documentary cinematographer and erstwhile amateur historian, wrote his greatest masterpiece with his own blood. He joined the ranks of cinematography's greatest anti-heroes: Dickens' Sydney Carton who went to the guillotine for someone else, Bogart's Rick Blaine who stayed while his love went with the hero, and Beatty's John "Squeaky" McCabe who fought and died in the cold merciless snow for a lover, a lost snow-queen herself.

The sky turned dark and strong winds began buffeted the ship, like birds attacking a fox. Then it was deadly quiet.

When Shepfield did not reappear after the explosion, Gaby began screaming and calling his name. Following Shepfield's instructions, Tom tried to comfort her. He held her tight.

"Meu amor, where is he?" she wailed.

Waya, realizing their danger, said calmly, "We must go now. I will see to it. You two take care of this woman."

Martins appeared on deck, smiling down from the railing above them. Tom yelled, "Take us out of here, Waya, before the crew gets ideas." Tom did not know that only Martins was left. But Martins had a plan.

The Golden Day collaborator rushed to the rear Gatling gun, which faced the escaping boat. It was a two-man job, but he succeeded in loading the ammunition. Unfortunately, this was the same gun that had malfunctioned during the pirate attack. It would not operate, and Martins pounded on it in frustration. He ran to the captain's cabin. As he had never started the ship's engine, it took him some minutes to get her started. Unsure of how to steer the ship, he fumbled with the controls, causing the ship to veer right, then left. Once the vessel was moving forward, he saw that the escaping skiff was almost halfway to shore. Martins headed after them at full speed in an attempt to ram the smaller craft.

But Martins knew nothing about the ship's draft and the minimum depth of water in which the ship could navigate. By the time he reached the skiff, the water level had lowered substantially, and he ran the Olympia aground. He grabbed the ship's radio and alerted his Golden Day contact.

As Martins watched them reach the port, he reflected on his own uncertain future. He was of no further use to Black Sun, but maybe the fact he had the cruiser, albeit run aground, would make him of some use to them. He did not speak Portuguese but his Golden Day contact had spoken English. Maybe he could come out of this mess on top. The Brazilians would get the ship working again and maybe even make him the captain, if he could prove that he knew something about the boat.

Golden Day, believing that the trio's voyage had been planned by Cross and Crescent, had changed plans without informing Martins. They decided they would gain more by letting the trio travel to São Paulo. By observing the group surreptitiously, they could determine their contacts along the way. Their street surveillants were already in position around the town when the dinghy docked at the fisherman's wharf.

Chapter 35
The Barzinho do Porto

Moving slowly along the beach, the four survivors needed to find a place to eat and sleep before locating a ship that could take them south along the coast. Without thinking, Helene asked Gaby how they could contact her relatives. The poor girl was lost. Even if her mind had not been full of pain, sorrow and loss, there was little chance of contacting them. With the old city of Fortaleza under water and its citizens dead, survivors fled in many different directions. Gaby mechanically replied, "There is no way. It doesn't matter now. My love has gone like a bird to the sky and I'm so sozinha. All alone." She hummed the words of a haunting Brazilian melody, Onde está você agora?

Helene put her arm around the Brazilian girl's shoulder and said softly, "It's set then. You will come with us. We will take you to Brasilia where you will be safe. We can help each other. Your Portuguese will be invaluable. You're one of us now. We will protect you."

Tom looked Gaby straight in the eyes. "Shepfield's last wish was that I take care of you. I gave him my word I would do it. You can count on us. We need to get something to eat and drink, and find a place where we can make some plans. Suggestions, anyone?"

Gaby brushed the tears from her eyes and looked around. She pointed across the beach. "There's a pub over there. See it? It's called the Barzinho do Porto. We can get a beer and maybe some fish."

They left the beach and crossed a small dirt road lined with palm trees that ran along the beira mar. It connected the fishing wharf to the rest of the town and the mangrove swamp farther down the coast. It was a small town with a grassy square containing an outdoor market, a mayor's office and two churches, one Catholic and one crente, born-again Protestant. Beyond the square to the rear and farther inland were groves of Brazil nut trees, cajus, mangos, and guava fruit.

Unlike the former Fortaleza, there were no street stalls

like the ones that sold glass bottles filled with different colored sands that painted a sand-picture. There were no tourists to buy these. The dunes that had mesmerized tourists, where they had come to practice ski-bunda, sliding down the dunes on boards, or to jump from dune to dune on adrenaline pumping open jeep rides, had been swallowed by the sea. The Barzinho do Porto, looking almost abandoned, sat at the northeast corner where the square met the beira mar.

When they walked into the run-down wooden building, Gaby greeted the owner. "Oi, Tudo bem. Quatro para comer, por favor. Vocês tem cerveja e peixe?"

The owner nodded in the affirmative. He had fish, beer, and a table for four. He motioned for them to take the open seats at a metal table with rusty chairs. The table was next to a dirty glass window that stretched along the front of the bar and allowed them a foggy view of the sea.

After the beer arrived, Tom asked the waiter in English if the beers were cold. Gabby translated the question and the waiter's response. "He says that if it is windy, he puts the bottle in a wet sock and hangs it on a line in the shade where the wind can blow through it. Today there was no wind, so he took them from the bottles he had stored in his cellar."

Looking at the other three, Tom said, "I'd like to make a toast. To friends we lost along the way. Those who made it possible for us to be here." Looking at the Cherokee, he said, "Waya, it is a tradition to honor the dead, and you must drink each time a toast is proposed."

The Cherokee quickly picked up his beer and looked at the others. "Though she is not dead, I will celebrate Mrs. Burk," he said. He drank and slammed his bottle on the table.

"Who is this Mrs. Burk?" Gaby asked.

"She is a friend, more than that, a role model," Helene replied. "I used to think that all that was real was what I could see and touch—biology, chemistry—the world was a mess and revenge all we had. Mrs. Burk showed me that there can be more than that. There is love." She raised her bottle. "To Mary Burk, may your God protect and preserve you, wherever you are."

Tom commented pensively. "I think she let us save her. After seeing her quell the storm at sea, I'm sure she could have saved herself from that firing squad. I think she gave us a chance to save ourselves. Look at you, Waya. You listened to your Great Spirit and avoided killing that soldier when you had the chance.

"I'm not sure what I believe. Cross and Crescent's

philosophers believe we substitute evil thoughts in our minds with good and restore the world, but their followers in America fight force with force. Mrs. Burk told us that evil is always defeated by recognizing its powerlessness. Waya's people believe that man can open the windows of heaven, harmony can return, and we can avoid the end of the world."

"You are right, Tom," Waya said. "Mrs. Burk and my people both share a belief in the Great Spirit, the one and only creator who is good. But I can't follow her methods. I think we must fight evil. Now, I'm not sure. Maybe what she believes works as well?"

Gaby added, "Marian told us that her people, the Arawak, believe the Spirit World, from which we all come, is the real world. But where is that world now?"

Tom raised his bottle again and said, "Let's not forget Josh and Antoine, two courageous soldiers and friends. May they continue to fight the battle so that good can prevail."

Helene's right hand shook, and she covered her eyes with her left. Then she raised her bottle. "To Antoine. Thanks for showing me Albert Camus. His words are locked in my heart." In a trembling voice almost inaudible, she repeated the words, "In the depth of winter there lies within us an invincible summer. I think Shepfield found his invincible summer. First, the way he handled those pirates, then when the crew rebelled.

"He sacrificed his life for us, *for all of us*."

Seeing Gaby tear up again, Tom ended the toast. He pulled his ragged New Testament from his jeans pocket and opened it at random. The book opened to Corinthians. He read the passage aloud. "In a moment, in the twinkling of an eye, at the last trump: for the trumpet shall sound, and the dead shall be raised incorruptible, and we shall be changed." He closed the book and put it away.

"Let's find a place to sleep," he said. "Tomorrow we'll locate a boat, sail to São Paulo, and go overland to Brasilia." It seemed so simple when he put it that way.

The Golden Day surveillant, selling fresh coconuts at the stand across the square from the bar, verified his cover was still intact. They had not spotted him. His colorful t-shirt that extended over the top of his shorts hid the pistol stuck in the back of his leather belt. He planned to ask the boss for an old-fashioned battery run Motorola-type handheld walkie talkie. The old technology did not depend on the now non-existent cell towers.

He would also ask for more men. Perhaps a team of

five. The whole thing needed to be discreet. He thought, *I'd love to get my hands on those two garotas. The girls would be a nice diversion from my hard life. Maybe I can follow them to wherever they were headed. Maybe the boss will let me participate in the interrogation when the time comes.*

He waved his hand in the air to signal to his replacement positioned beside the church that he was leaving. Claudio could take over the watch. He left the coconuts on the wooden stand and slowly began to walk toward the town hall where his HQ was located. The boss would be happy with his report. Tomorrow, he would watch them again.

They needed to be stopped—these traitors who defied the new order. It was all that counted. Not aware that they were under surveillance, the travelers discussed their next steps in the continued quest to find the Cross and Crescent.

THE END

The saga continues in the next book,
"Twinkling of an Eye".
Will our heroes arrive in Brasilia?
Can they save the world?
Or are they destined to fight a losing battle for
themselves and humanity?

About the Author

Christian Pascale is a writer and a poet who was born in Brooklyn, New York. He graduated from Lafayette College Magna Cum Lauda with degrees in French and International Relations. At Lafayette, he was inducted into the Phi Beta Kappa honor society and then went on to receive an M.A. in European Area Studies from American University in Washington D.C. and a Doctorat de l'université from La Sorbonne in Paris, France. During his early years, he worked as a substitute teacher, a tennis instructor in Europe and the U.S., a teacher of English as a Foreign Language, a political fundraiser, and Director of Studies at a New England preparatory school. For more than thirty years, he worked in both domestic and foreign assignments for the United States Government.

Christian has published twenty poems in internationally distributed magazines and is the author of *Poetry of Wonder*, a book of poems. He is a member of the James City Poets and Chesapeake Bay Writers. He is married to Liria Hoffmann Pascale who is a native Brazilian and an architect. They live in Williamsburg, Virginia and have two adult sons.

He can be found at christianpascale.com.